PRAISE FOR JAMES SCOTT BELL

A master of the cliffhanger, creating scene after scene of mounting suspense and revelation . . . Heart-whamming.

— **PUBLISHERS WEEKLY**

A master of suspense.

— **LIBRARY JOURNAL**

One of the best writers out there, bar none.

— **IN THE LIBRARY REVIEW**

There'll be no sleeping till after the story is over.

— **JOHN GILSTRAP**, NYT
BESTSELLING AUTHOR

James Scott Bell's series is as sharp as a switchblade.

— **MEG GARDINER**, EDGAR AWARD
WINNING AUTHOR

One of the top authors in the crowded suspense genre.

— **SHELDON SIEGEL**, NYT
BESTSELLING AUTHOR

ROMEO'S TOWN

A Mike Romeo Thriller

JAMES SCOTT BELL

Compendium Press

ISBN: 978-0-910355-54-4

Compendium Press
Woodland Hills, CA

Lord, what fools these mortals be!

— PUCK, A MIDSUMMER NIGHT'S
DREAM

People sleep peacefully in their beds at night only because rough men stand ready to do violence on their behalf.

— GEORGE ORWELL

ROMEO'S TOWN

Two minutes before the knife attack I was sitting on a folding chair outside the Odysseus Bookstore in downtown L.A. Yep, an independent bookstore had managed to survive lockdowns, street riots, arson, and general fear o' the virus. Wounded though it was, with boards on the windows, it was at long last doing some business again.

I know the owner of Odysseus, a middle-aged bibliophile named Tony. An anonymous donor had given the store a much-needed infusion of cash. That still left it hanging. Even in good times a bookstore is a thin-margin business. A combo new-and-used bookstore is an endangered retail species. I was glad to be giving it what business I could. I'm all for preserving bookstores, pandas, and the blue-footed booby.

So there I was, leafing through a used hardback of Harold Bloom's *Shakespeare: The Invention of the Human*. I'm always interested in what the scholars say about Iago. The guy has some of the best lines in Shakespeare, and even though he's a complete turd, he sometimes says wise things like, "If the balance of our lives had not one scale of reason to poise another of sensuality, the blood and baseness of our natures would conduct us to most preposterous conclusions." We see that truth played out every day now. Reason is long gone. Balance and restraint are quaint vestiges of the past. We're a world of blood and baseness, full of Iagos, a character—Bloom says—with "great intellectual activity, accompanied with a total want of moral principle."

Welcome to our current politics.

But I digress.

I looked up from the book and saw a guy dressed in a dirty green jacket. He was about my size, six-four, white, wearing a black gaiter mask. I wouldn't have paid him any attention except for one thing—he pulled a knife out of his jacket pocket. A six-inch blade, at least. He flipped it in his hand so his forearm hid the blade, and headed into the bookstore.

So did I.

The guy made for the counter. Behind it was a young woman named Wanda. She was looking down at something.

Knife Guy was going to cut her. It was the way he held the knife, the tightness of his fist, the purposeful walk. He wasn't going there to ask where the poetry section was.

In a spot like that you can't hesitate. I would have taken him down myself but there was a little too much space between us at the critical moment.

In a pinch, an 800-page hardback makes a useful weapon. If you know how to throw it, that is. Fling it haphazardly and it's liable to fly open and lose all force as the pages riffle in the air. The key is to hold it with the spine facing you, and hurl it so it makes only one revolution, like an ax.

How do I know this? Because I used to throw books across my dorm room at Yale when I found too many stupid utterances in them. But you can be pretty intellectually arrogant when you're fifteen years old.

I threw Harold Bloom at the side of the guy's head.

The sharp points of the cover nailed him just above the neck. He went down like a garbage bag tossed in a dumpster.

Wanda looked up.

A man standing at a paperback spinner said, "Whoa!"

Knife Guy rolled on the ground. I put a knee on his back and grabbed his wrist, slammed it on the floor a couple of times. The knife came loose. I pulled his arm behind him and pinned it with my knee. I picked up the knife and put it on the counter.

"Call the police," I said.

Wanda was already on the phone.

Knife Guy started cursing. I tweaked his skull and told him to shut up. There were children in the store.

A woman watching from the fringe said, "That's brutality!"

I had no words.

"And where is your mask?" she said. "You're not wearing a mask!"

I started having bad thoughts.

Tony stepped in and said to the customers, "Come on, now. Let's back away."

"This store isn't safe!" the angry woman said.

"We have two exits, ma'am," Tony said.

Knife Guy screamed something profane. I grabbed his hair, pulled his head up, and said, "Not another word."

He gave me another word.

I slammed his head on the floor. Not enough to put him to sleep. I know my own strength. He screamed a few other profanities.

"Stop it!" the angry woman said. "Just stop it right now!"

"Stop what?" I said. "This?"

I slammed his head again. This time Knife Guy didn't say anything.

"I am going to tell the police what you've done!" the woman said.

Bad thoughts returned.

I stood and put my foot on Knife Guy's back. Wanda had finished her call and her arms were crossed in front of her. She was shaking.

"You okay?" I said.

"I don't know," Wanda said. She was around twenty-five, went to Cal State Northridge. We'd had some friendly conversations before.

Tony went behind the counter and put his arm around Wanda. "Come sit down, wait for the police. I'll get you some water."

The angry woman took out her phone and pointed it at me. The phone as weapon. I'll show you! I can take your picture and show it to the police or put it on the internet forever! And I hope it ruins your life!

This is what the long, slow crawl to civilization has come to. The great unraveling is here, and it seems unstoppable.

Five or six minutes later a pair of cops arrived. A man and a woman. The woman's name plate said *Ortega*. Through her mask she asked me what I was doing, since I was sitting on Knife Guy.

I said, "This guy came at Ms. Young." I nodded toward Wanda, who was sitting behind the counter. "He had a knife. I stopped him. The knife is on the counter."

The officer asked Wanda if what I said was accurate. Wanda nodded.

Then that woman stepped in. "He was hitting this man's head on the ground! You should arrest *him*."

Officer Ortega seemed to have a natural nutcase meter, and put her hands out. "All right, everyone, just calm down."

She leaned over Knife Guy. "Sir, I'm going to ask you to come with us until this is straightened out."

Knife Guy let her know what he thought of that idea. Also that he knew his rights, and that he was going to sue the police. This did not endear him to the officers. The male officer attempted to place handcuffs on Knife Guy. Knife Guy fought him from the ground. The officer seemed reluctant to apply any force. That's how it is these days, especially with camera phones all around.

So I grabbed Knife Guy's hair and gave his head a healthy pound on the floor.

"It helps if you do that," I said.

A fter they got the woozy attacker in the car, Officer Ortega interviewed me by the biography section.

"You were the one who subdued the suspect?"

"Yes."

"What made you do it?"

"His knife."

"You saw it?"

"He was going to cut the woman at the counter."

"And you knew this how?"

"The cut of his jib."

"The what?"

"I could tell by his body language what he intended to do. You don't approach someone with a knife held against your forearm unless you mean to use it."

"You were taking an awful chance."

"On the scale of awful, I err on the side of keeping someone alive."

"If you don't mind, a detective will be here soon and I

know he'll want to talk to you."

"Would it matter if I do mind?"

"No."

"Then I'll be over in the mystery section."

The lead detective's name was Coltrane Smith. He was in his forties, medium height, wearing a mask, coat, open-collared shirt, and a shield on his belt. His partner was a woman named Jenson. Smith handled my statement. I went over the same ground as I did with the officer.

"I get it," Smith said. "But it's going to be hard to make out assault with a deadly when there wasn't any assault."

"You don't call walking up to someone with a knife an assault?" I said.

"You're the only one who saw it, looks like. The intended victim, if she was that, didn't see him coming."

"Then charge him with an about-to-be-an-assault," I said.

I think Smith may have smiled. "If only."

"You should at least get him on the knife."

Smith nodded. "If he's got a record, maybe ex-felon with a weapon. If we need you, you'll testify, yes?"

"Sure."

"The only other thing..."

"Is?"

"What's this about you pounding his head on the ground?"

"I believe that's called subduing a dangerous suspect."

"Wasn't he under your control when you did that?"

"He was assaulting the customers, including children, with words."

"Words?"

"Bad words. I put a stop to it."

"You pounded this guy's head because he was cursing?"

"I'm a sensitive sort."

Smith shook his head. "That's a new one."

"I gave him one more when he was fighting your officers trying to cuff him."

After a couple of eye blinks, Detective Coltrane Smith said, "Here's my card. What's the best way to get in touch with you?"

I pulled out one of Ira's cards and gave it to him. "Through my lawyer-employer."

Smith scratched the back of his head. "We'll have to see how this plays out. These days it's, well, not a good move to go too rough on an arrestee."

"I didn't arrest him," I said.

"It may complicate a prosecution."

"What's life without complications?"

"Stuff happens," Smith said.

"Fate," I said.

"I don't believe in fate."

"Neither do I," I said.

That's when fate entered the bookstore.

The Greeks attributed everything that happens to three goddesses who create the warp and woof of our lives. Clotho works on a spinning wheel. Lachesis measures out thread. But it is Atropos who has the ultimate power. She holds the shears and can cut wherever she pleases.

So all the terrible outcomes of life could be attributed to these spin sisters, the Three Fates. It was a way of explaining the bad stuff. But they tossed in a bone of goodness now and again, just to keep things sporting. When fate happens, you don't always know if it will be for ultimate good, ultimate evil, or something in between.

We don't buy into the myth anymore, of course. But when certain things happen I wonder if I hear the creak of a spinning wheel in some dark corner of the cosmos. Or sense the noiseless hand of God. As the Hebrews put it in their holy book: *The lot is cast into the lap. But the whole disposing thereof is of the Lord.*

Whatever the attribution of stuff that happens—in Detective Coltrane Smith's words—I was gobsmacked when Sophie Montag walked into the Odysseus Bookstore.

T he only woman I ever loved looked as beautiful as ever, even with a mask on her face. Tall, sunset-red hair, intelligent eyes behind black-frame glasses, dressed in jeans and a white sweatshirt with *Constantine Academy* stenciled on the front. The orchestra in me that had been sitting around for months suddenly sat up and began a Beethoven symphony.

"Mike!" she said.

"Sophie," I said.

"What ..." She looked around. "What's happened here?"

"We had a little commotion."

She looked knowingly at me.

"It always seems to happen when I read Harold Bloom," I said.

"You're going to have to explain that one to me."

"You want me to?"

After a moment's hesitation, she said, "Yes."

W e decided to take a walk. Which is to take a risk in downtown L.A. Four blocks from the store was Skid Row. Not your grandfather's Skid Row, where derelicts and winos and transients would sleep in doorways and curbsides until rousted by cops and taken to a facility for a 72-hour hold.

No more rousting. No more holds.

It's a haven for meth and heroin addicts living in tents and boxes, undisturbed by a police force that's been told to stand down. If you can avoid the rats you'll see men smoking meth in the afternoon sun, women selling bootleg cigs on top of cardboard boxes or trading sex for money. Men flashing dope to passing cars. That old man slumped in the doorway of an abandoned garment business? He's shooting heroin into his cracked, bare feet.

Take a wide swath around the Row, and you'll find boarded-up buildings, the wounds of the looting and riots that choked the city last summer while the fat cats in City Hall preened for the cameras.

We headed toward Pershing Square, weaving our way past the pedestrians on Broadway and the cars on Hill. We found a bench where we had a view of the classic Biltmore Hotel, the last place the famous Black Dahlia was seen alive. Los Angeles is a city of ghosts, some in black and white, some in color. Pershing Square itself is like that. Designed to be the city's "Central Park," it is now mostly a slab of concrete with multi-colored protuberances, sitting on top of an underground parking garage.

It wouldn't be a place I'd spend ten seconds, but with Sophie I didn't care about time. She took off her mask. Perfect lips to go with those eyes. The Beethoven symphony in my chest swelled into *allegro con brio*.

I quickly came up with something original to say. "What are you doing these days?"

"Teaching," Sophie said. "Seventh grade English."

"At The Constantine Academy?"

She looked astonished. "How did you know that?"

I tapped my head. "There are not many things in this town I don't know about. Plus, it's on your sweatshirt."

She looked down and laughed. "I forgot all about it. And here I was starting to think you were truly gifted."

It was good to hear that from her, the easy banter, the way it had once been with us.

I said, "It sounds pricey and private."

"It is," she said. "But you'll like this, it's a classical curriculum."

"A classical school in Los Angeles? I'm stunned."

"I know."

"They'll be coming after you, you know."

"Who?"

"The torches and pitchforks crowd."

A fleeting look of sadness came to her then.

"Which makes you a hero in my book," I said. "Don't give up the fight."

"You ought to stop by sometime," she said.

"You're meeting onsite?"

"Just starting to. And the kids would love to hear what a real, live private eye does."

"Not PI," I said. "You need a license for that. I'm an investigator for a lawyer."

"That's just as cool."

"Then there's hope for the future," I said.

"Are you up to it?"

Before we went on, something needed to be cleared up. "As I recall," I said, "you weren't too thrilled that I put the hurt on your boyfriend."

She looked at her hands. "Ex-boyfriend."

"Right," I said.

"I've thought a lot about what happened," she said.

"If it helps, I'm sorry it did."

"No," she said. "I understand why you did it. I told you

about my father, how he used to hit my mother. How I tried to stop him once and got hit myself. He left us after that. But I remember at that moment, I did want to stop him, using any means I could."

"There's nothing wrong with that," I said. "Not in my philosophy, anyway."

"I guess I'm still trying to work it all out."

"That's good," I said. "Not many people are interested in working things out anymore. Philosophically speaking."

"So," Sophie said, "let's arrange a guest appearance."

I wanted to see her again. And I didn't. There was a murky fog ahead and I didn't want to crash into a mountain. And bring her down with me. But as Pascal said, the heart has its reasons which reason knows nothing of.

"Okay," I said. "Why don't we—"

My phone buzzed. It was Ira.

"Excuse me," I said. "I have to take this."

Sophie nodded.

"Ira," I said.

"Michael, where are you?"

"I'm downtown, sitting with a friend."

"Can you meet me at the juvenile detention center on Eastlake?"

"When?"

"Half an hour. We have a client."

"I'll be there."

I put the phone away and said, "Looks like I have to go to work."

"It was nice running into you," Sophie said. "Though the circumstances were certainly unique."

"I do want to visit your class," I said. "Can I call you to arrange something?"

"Please."

I liked the way she said that.

"How'd you get down here?" I asked.

"Subway," she said.

"Can I walk you to the station?"

"That'd be nice," she said.

"I'm working on that," I said.

"On what?"

"Being nice."

She laughed then, and it was a good laugh. Pure as the air at Paradise Cove. We walked up Hill Street. It was eerie, what with all the businesses closed down. What should have been a bustling Central Market was now more like a cemetery with two or three funerals going on.

At the subway entrance we paused for a moment. I put out my hand like some doofus insurance salesman. Sophie shook it. If the angry lady at the bookstore had seen that, she would have screamed bloody murder.

Central Juvenile Hall is a long, ugly, one-story warehouse for what they used to call "wayward kids." Row upon row of 8x12 rooms for minors incarcerated for various offenses, or awaiting their day in court. Juvenile law is its own system. Originally, it was set up with the thought that kids—overwhelmingly boys—do stupid things that sometimes end up in criminal acts. Instead of dumping them in prison, the theory went, let's give them a break and time to mature and learn some discipline. Then they can become productive adults.

But that theory is being severely tested now, as kids become more violent earlier, doing things as a twelve-year-old that would have been unthinkable a generation ago. Why is that? Why aren't consciences being developed as in the past? It's not hard to figure out if you really want the answers. But not everyone does. A depressingly large contingent doesn't want to hear about the crisis of father-lessness and the erosion of values like study, hard work, and respect for elders.

Ira calls me a young dinosaur.

So I couldn't help wondering what kind of kid our client was going to be.

I joined Ira in the attorney interview room. These days most lawyers meet with clients via video. Ira prefers it to be in person. We were both wearing the required face masks—Ira carries extras for me. We sat at a table with a Plexiglass separator. Ira took out a file.

"His name is Clint Cunningham," Ira said. "Sixteen. His mother used to attend my synagogue. She called me last night."

"What's he been arrested for?" I asked.

"Dealing drugs."

"Terrific. What kind?"

"We don't know yet. Whatever it was, his mother insists he's doing it under some kind of duress."

"Naturally."

"I believe her."

"You believe that's what she believes," I said.

"Is that a crack?"

"You like to see the best in people."

"Is that why I put up with you?" Ira said.

"That," I said, "and the fact that I *am* the best."

Ira closed his eyes and shook his head. I think he prays for me when he does that.

The door opened and a deputy sheriff led Clint Cunningham into the attorney room. The kid was a chunk, had big eyes peeking over his mask, and messy, shoulder-length brown hair. He wore a dull gray T-shirt a size too small, black sweatpants, tennis shoes. The deputy sat him on the bench on the other side of the Plexiglas.

"Ten minutes," the deputy said, then left the room.

Clint Cunningham's eyes, big as they were, had a deadness to them. Kids his age should have eyes that gleam and ask and demand and laugh, with an occasional dance thrown in. His were empty warehouses at midnight. Maybe once there were items inside—favorite toys, a bike, a first suit and tie. Now there was nothing but dark space and cobwebs.

"Clint, my name is Ira. This is Mike."

Clint's expression, what we could see of it, didn't change.

Ira said, "Your mother asked us to talk to you. I'm a lawyer. I'll be handling your case."

"Why?" Clint said in a flat, distant voice.

"Because you're being charged with a serious crime. You need help."

He shook his head. "I did it."

"Well now, we'll need to talk about that," Ira said. "What I want for you, what your mother wants, is what's best for your future."

"Prison," Clint said.

"You're not going to prison," Ira said. "You're a juvenile and a first-time offender. But the facts of the case matter. Why don't we go through them step by step?"

"They gonna keep me here?"

"For now," Ira said. "I'll arrange a hearing as soon as possible to see if we can get you out. Now, how about telling us what's been going on, from the beginning of things."

"Beginning?" Clint said.

"How you got involved in selling drugs, if that's what you were doing."

"I already told you I was."

The kid sure seemed anxious to cop to the crime. But

not out of any sense of remorse. I tried to read his face, but the mask made it next to impossible.

Ira said, "Tell us how it started then."

Clint looked at the table.

"I can't help you if you don't work with me," Ira said.

"I don't need you," Clint said.

"You're wrong, kid," I said. That just popped out, and it came with a wave of feeling I wasn't prepared for.

Ira quieted me with a hand on my arm. To Clint he said, "Won't you give me chance? I've worked with kids your age before. I'm happy to say they're all doing much better now. Sometimes you just need a break in life, and a chance to start over."

Our client—if he was our client—stayed silent.

"Tell you what," Ira said. "I'll have a talk with the prosecutor, right after I leave. Let's see what she's willing to do. We might be able to settle this thing quick, and get you out on probation. That's a lot better than jail time, don't you think?"

Clint didn't indicate a thing.

"We'll be back to talk, okay?" Ira said.

Clint kept looking at the table.

Ira and I walked to the parking structure. Ira was using his arm braces today, rather than his wheelchair. The wound he'd received years ago as a Mossad agent mandated that he use one or the other.

"What did you observe?" Ira asked.

"Somebody's pressuring him not to talk," I said.

"His supplier?"

"Most likely."

"Let's take it step by step," Ira said. "Start by interviewing his mother."

He gave me the address. It was in the Valley.

"When I called you," Ira said, "you said you were with a friend."

"Sophie."

"Ah, from the bookstore."

"A chance encounter," I said.

"Or Divine Providence," Ira said.

"It's time to say goodbye, Ira."

"Don't keep running from human connections."

"How about if I just walk fast?" I said, and headed for my green Mustang convertible, Spinoza.

I hopped on the 10 heading west. Sunday traffic was nice and light and the sun was starting its leisurely swan dive into the Pacific. It only took twenty minutes to get to the good old Pacific Coast Highway. Half an hour after that I pulled into Paradise Cove. I couldn't wait to get into the chop for a swim. The weather was cool, the water bracing. I parked Spinoza in my spot in front of the mobile unit Ira owns and where I live. It's cozy and I breathe the same air as the billionaires on Broad Beach.

Bim, bam and I was on the beach, running to the water, diving into a wave. But I couldn't stop thinking about Clint Cunningham. How he reminded me of me. I'd been a pudgy, cerebral, so-called genius who got admitted to Yale at age fifteen. That's the definition of an outsider. I didn't even binge drink. My only poison was Dr. Pepper. And girls? Forget about it. I was a plump insect in their terrarium, an object to look at with curiosity, but never to touch.

After twenty minutes or so I body-surfed a wave all the way to the sand. It was one of those rare perfect rides you get from time to time. It delivered me softly, like a mother putting a sleeping baby in a crib.

"Nice ride, dude."

C Dog was standing on the dry sand. Carter "C Dog" Weeks is a twenty-something rocker with his own band, Unopened Cheese. He's also a recovering pothead. I've been trying to help him use his brain, which has been mostly awash in a cannabis fog for the last several years. He's been responding positively.

Except now. He was wearing a mask.

"Take that thing off," I said.

"Whu—?"

"You're outside! And alone."

"You're here."

"Am I in your face? Take that thing off and breathe free air."

Sheepishly, he slid the mask off. "I was only—"

"I know what you were only. Have a seat."

He dropped to the sand. I picked up my towel and started drying off.

I said, "Did you read the book?"

"Yeah, I did."

"Now that is a good thing, isn't it?"

He nodded.

"So what did you think?" I said.

"Think?"

"It's called literary analysis."

"Oh man."

"Let's just start with this. What was it about?"

Brow furrowed, C Dog said, "Well, it's about this old man who hasn't had luck fishing, and he goes way out and has this fight with a big fish. Epic. Finally he gets it, ties it to his boat. But sharks come along and eat it. So all he has left is bones. Which bites the cosmic dog, man."

"I think I know what you mean," I said.

"So what's the point?"

"What do you think it is?"

"I don't know!"

"Yes, you do. You just don't realize it yet." I tapped the side of my head. "Think!"

He looked up at the sky. Then down at the sand. "Life pretty much sucks."

"Why?"

"Sharks."

I nodded. "Do you know what symbolism is?"

"Sort of. Something is supposed to be something else."

"Let's suppose sharks are a symbol," I said. "What is the something else?"

He thought about it, then earnestly replied, "A symbol that life sucks?"

"Leave life aside for a moment," I said. "What do the sharks do?"

"Eat fish and people sometimes."

"What did Santiago do for a living?"

"Fished."

"Let's say somebody is a doctor. Or a lawyer. Or a rocker."

"I'll take rocker!"

"Are there things or people who will try to eat your work? Destroy it?"

His eyes widened a little. "Oh yeah, I think I see what you're saying."

I said, "What if you got arthritis in your hands. Would you stop playing guitar?"

"No way, man."

"You wouldn't give it up?"

"There is absolutely no way. Not my guitar."

"That's the lesson here," I said. "There is something noble and heroic in not giving up. And that is why, at the end, Santiago could have his dream of the lions."

For a long moment the only sound was the waves lapping the beach.

Then C Dog said, "Wow."

"And that," I said, "is literary analysis."

He nodded. "Awesome."

"How about a beer, my friend?" I said.

"Absolutely," he said.

We went back to my place and I got out a couple of Coronas. I cut two wedges from a lime and stuck them in the bottles. We sat on the porch and drank and watched the big orange ball sink.

I couldn't stop thinking about sharks.

Monday morning I drove out to Studio City to talk to Clint's mother. The neighborhood got its name back in the 1920s when a silent comedy producer named Mack Sennett built a studio in this part of the San Fernando Valley. As houses sprung up around it, they decided to call the place Studio City. Sennett was known for originating slapstick, which is a perfect way to describe the politics of this town.

Trista Cunningham's home was on a nicely appointed street called Bellingham. It was a sky-blue house with white trim and a yellow front door. It had a neatly clipped front lawn and a hedge along the driveway. There was a trellis just off the front porch with a hearty spread of nasturtiums. I'm a fan of this genus, especially the "flame thrower" variety as these were. The yellow, scarlet and orange petals are optimistic and merry—two things sorely lacking in the dismal weeds of contemporary society.

I knocked on the door and Trista Cunningham answered. She was in her late thirties, smallish, with short brown hair. She was wearing a flowered shirtdress with an open lapel collar, and big side pockets.

"I'm Mike," I said.

"Thanks for coming over," she said.

"Would you like me to wear a mask?"

"Not at all," she said.

I immediately took a liking to this woman.

"Can I offer you some coffee?" she said.

"Absolutely," I said.

There was a dining room table near the front window with a computer and lots of papers stacked around it. As she poured the coffee she said, "Please excuse the mess. I'm working on a big project and don't have a filing system here at the house."

"No problem."

"I manage inventory for a fresh produce company."

"Oh? What kind of produce?"

"Blueberries, mostly. We're headquartered here in L.A. We've got warehouse operations here and in New Jersey. We also operate a blueberry packinghouse in Aurora, Oregon."

"So basically you keep track of berries."

She smiled and handed me a cup of coffee. "You could put it that way." She was trying for easy, casual conversation but you couldn't miss the crush of anxiety just below the surface.

We sat in the living room.

"How does he look?" Trista asked.

"Like a kid his age would look in these circumstances," I said. "Scared, trying not to show it."

"They won't let me see him. That's inhuman."

"It is," I said. "There's a lot of that going around these days."

She looked at her coffee.

I said, "Let me assure you that Ira Rosen is a great

lawyer and we'll do everything we can to get Clint the right disposition."

"What happens next?" Trista asked.

"An initial hearing before a judge. At that time the judge is going to ask for a plea or see if a plea deal has been worked out."

"What about a trial?"

"Clint insists he wants to enter a plea. That would mean no trial. But he should be given a light sentence, considering it's his first offense. No jail time. Except..."

"Except what?"

"The Deputy D.A. may not consider a plea bargain unless Clint gives up his supplier. We think that's why Clint isn't saying anything. He may be facing pressure from the outside."

Trista put her cup on the coffee table and then her head in her hands. "I don't know how it got to this."

"Tell me about his schooling," I said.

She lifted her head, took a breath to compose herself. "He goes to private school, Elias Hall. It's almost bankrupting me."

"Why not public school?"

"L.A public school? Are you kidding? Clint is smart. Tests almost genius level. But he's insecure about it. He's always been the youngest in his classes and got picked on a lot. I thought Elias would be better for him."

"I understand," I said

"Do you? You don't look like you ever got picked on."

"I'll tell you something. I was a pudgy smart kid, too. I know all about hazing and demoralization."

"You were pudgy?" she said with a slight smile.

"A butterball," I said.

"Good heavens, look at you now."

"I try not to," I said. It was supposed to be a flippant

remark, but the moment I said it I realized I meant it in a deeper way. I pulled myself out of the deep and said, "How has he gotten along in the new school?"

"It started out well," she said. "Last year he got a little more life in him. Seemed happier. He had a girlfriend for the first time in his life."

"Do you know if he was doing drugs?"

Trista Cunningham shook her head. "I don't think so. Not that I could tell. But he probably was. They all do, don't they?"

"Not all."

"More than my generation," she said. "But I'm not that far removed. I had Clint when I was twenty."

"His father involved?"

"Barely. We've been divorced ten years. He didn't fight for joint custody. Used to see Clint once or twice a month. He's dropped off lately."

"I should talk to him."

"Good luck with that," she said.

"Hard to find?"

"Hard to talk to."

"Name?"

"Brian."

"What would be the best way to contact him?"

"Holding a crowbar," she said, then laughed at herself. "I'm sorry. I sound bitter, don't I?"

"The bitterness of my mind urges me at all hazards to speak what I think."

She gave me a quizzical look.

"Thomas Becket," I said.

"Who?"

"Archbishop of Canterbury, twelfth century." I tapped my head. "Quotes jump out from time to time."

"What did he mean?"

"Sometimes it's best to let the bitterness of the truth out so it can be dealt with in broad daylight."

"What was he bitter about?"

"The king. King Henry II. He wanted Becket to sign a document that gave the king powers over the church, and he told the king where he could stick it."

"Really?"

"Not in those words, exactly."

"So what happened?"

"Eventually, the king had enough. One day he was sitting around and shouted 'Will no one rid me of this meddlesome priest?' Some knights heard that and went and found Becket at prayer, and hacked him to death."

Trista Cunningham said, "Terrific."

"There are no kings around, Trista. So what can you tell me about Brian's relationship with Clint?"

"Distant," she said, and shook her head.

"What's the best way to contact him?"

"He won't want to talk to you. He never liked to talk, period. He's suspicious of everybody. If you had to get to him, I think it would be best to go to one of his jobsites. He does drywall. Has his own business, Cunningham Drywall. But I never know where he's working."

"There may be a way to find out."

We paused then and sipped some coffee.

I said, "What happened with that girl he was with?"

"She broke it off. It really hurt Clint. That's probably when all this started."

"Do you have her contact information?"

She took out her phone and scrolled. "Bianca Aiken." She gave me a phone number and an address. Then said, "Realistically, what will happen to Clint?"

"There are programs available to minors to deal with problems involving drugs, mental health issues, that kind of thing. But he's going to have to cooperate with us and the D.A. That may take some convincing."

"Convince him," she said. "He's all I've got."

"One other thing," I said. "The police may serve a search warrant here."

"Oh no."

"I should have a look at Clint's room."

"Are you...are we..."

"Allowed to do that?"

She nodded.

"Of course," I said, being almost sure of the legal part. "If I find anything I'll turn it over to Ira as attorney-client privilege material. He can sort out the legalities later. He's a very smart lawyer."

"I know," Trista said. "He saved my mother's house from foreclosure."

"Why don't you do some more work on your project, and I'll have a look at Clint's room?"

"Down the hall, first door on the left."

Clint's room was neat and tidy, like it had been made up as a guest room waiting for a guest. That had to be Trista's doing. The room had a mirrored closet, and next to that a nightstand. The nightstand had a lamp on it in the shape of an alien head. And something that looked like a wireless phone charger. The bed was twin size, with a brown comforter and two pillows—one regular pillow with a white cover, and one smaller pillow with a black cover and yellow lettering spelling out BE COOL.

Over the bed, tacked on the wall, was a Spider-Man poster.

On the wall opposite the bed was a big screen TV and a dresser. A game console sat on top of the dresser. Next to the dresser were some shelves holding books, DVDs, and a castle made of Legos.

The desk had a MacBook Air and gooseneck desk lamp. A straight-back chair was tucked up against the desk.

I sat in the chair and went through the three drawers in the desk. The top drawer was a mess of papers, sticky notes, pens, pencils, paperclips, a little stapler, some highlighters, and a Swiss Army Knife. The middle drawer had a harmonica and an instruction book—*Instant Blues Harmonica*. I tried not to picture Clint sitting in prison and blowing *Swing Low, Sweet Chariot* like in an old Warner Bros. movie.

The bottom drawer was locked.

Naturally I had to look inside.

My lock-picking skills are legendary in my own mind, all owing to Joey Feint's patient instruction. Joey Feint was a quirky New Haven private investigator I worked for back in the day, after my parents were murdered. He taught me some useful things. Like a rudimentary drawer lock being the proverbial piece of cake. I got two paperclips from the top drawer and straightened them, then twisted one into an L shape with a little hook to act as a tension wrench. I put the wrench in the lock. The Joey Feint secret is to put the tension wrench at the top of the lock instead of the bottom. I did and turned it clockwise until I felt the tension, then inserted the straight clip underneath, raking the pins. In two seconds the drawer was unlocked.

There were two three-ring binders in the drawer.

One had Spider-Man on the cover. Inside this one were plastic pages that held cards. Marvel trading cards mostly. A lot of Spidey, of course, but also Iron Man, Captain America, Hulk, Thor, Black Panther, Doctor Strange. Lovingly preserved.

The other binder, plain black cover, was thick with

notebook paper. The pages had writing on them, black ink. The writing was elegant, like calligraphy. Poems. Each page had a date at the bottom, and the initials CC.

I scanned a few of the pages. A poem from three years ago went like this:

I want to be the one you want
    I want to be the one you think
I want to be the one you see
I want to be the one you drink
All in all in all in all
In winter spring summer fall

Not exactly Robert Frost. But he was only thirteen when he wrote it.

Then this from two years ago:

Twisting, twisting, guts twisting
    no one listening no one listening
not god
not men
not women
not girls
not you

I went through a few more at random. There did appear to be a change in the poetry the further along in time. Not that it got better. It was more like entropy, an increasing degree of disorder.

The other notable point was that each poem had a

drawing with it. Clint was no poet, but he sure had artistic talent. I know, because I have none. My horses always come out looking like large, mutant dogs. Not so Clint Cunningham. He drew dense forests, birds of prey, medieval castles, exotic fish, superhero cars, and Spider-Man in various poses. All brilliant.

I kept reading. A year ago there was another change. The poems were now laced with profanity. There was no attempt to make the lines scan in any discernible way. And the drawings changed, too. They were bloody, horrific—Hallmark cards from hell.

The last page in the notebook had no writing at all. The entire page was an intricately designed death's head. Cracks in the cranium, mouth agape, teeth dripping with blood. A bony hand held a revolver pointed at the temple in what appeared to be an incipient act of skeleton suicide.

In the right eye socket, which was on the left side as you looked at the drawing, was a letter T. In the other was a B. In the mouth, a D.

Out of the D came a coiled snake, with bared fangs and fury in the eyes.

This page was dated a week ago.

For a long moment I sat there, just looking at it, wondering what it was trying to tell me about the insides of Clint Cunningham.

I put the Spider-Man binder back in the drawer.

I returned to the living room with the poetry notebook and the laptop.

Trista Cunningham was at her work station. "Did you find something?"

"Have you got a moment?" I said.

"Of course." She came over and sat next to me on the sofa. I held up the notebook.

"Did you ever see this before?"

"His school notebook?"

"His poetry."

She frowned. "That has poetry?"

"His attempts."

"Let me see." She put her hand out.

"I need to tell you, there are some disturbing things in here."

Her hand trembled a bit, but she kept it there. "I need to see."

I gave her the notebook. And watched for several minutes as she went through the pages.

"Things just keep getting better and better," she said.

"Trista, can I ask you to look at the last page?"

She opened to it. "Oh God." She turned her head and slammed the notebook shut.

"Sorry you had to see that," I said.

"TBD," she said softly. "To Be Done. I say that all the time. I have a pile on my desk with a TBD paperweight on it." She took a breath. "What do you think Clint means by it? With the gun..."

I didn't say what I thought.

She did. "That he's planning to kill himself."

A moment of silence, then she lowered her head. She looked like she was praying.

"I'll take this and the laptop to Ira," I said.

"And if the police come?" Trista said.

"If they don't have a warrant, they'll ask you for consent to search. Tell them on advice of your son's counsel you cannot give consent. If they do have a warrant, tell them you want to read it before they proceed. They have to give you a copy. There will be a page laying out exactly where they can search and what they can search for. It should be limited to Clint's room, perhaps his bathroom and the garage."

"What about my bedroom?"

"Absolutely not. Nor your workspace. If they ask to search there, tell them no, and give them Ira's phone number. If they try to anyway, call Ira right away."

"This is a nightmare," she said.

A nightmare that was just beginning.

"*This is a nightmare*" repeated in my mind as I drove to Bianca Aikens's address. It was in a section of Studio City called The Silver Triangle. South of the Boulevard, as they say, meaning Ventura Boulevard and the tonier neighborhoods that exist there. And if the prices are any indication, it's true. It's seven-figure territory.

The Aiken house was a two-story, Spanish-style home with a red, Mission-tile roof. I parked at the curb across the street. I was buttoning the top button of my Hawaiian shirt when a car varoomed up the street. Not just any car. A silver Porsche 911 Carrera convertible. A beautiful piece of machinery that had to cost at least a hundred-and-fifty large. It screeched to a stop in front of the Aiken house.

Behind the wheel was a guy in a red backward baseball cap. Next to him was a girl with short dark hair.

The driver jumped out. He wore a striped, button-up short-sleeve shirt, untucked over deep-blue slacks. His high-top basketball shoes were fire red and probably cost a couple hundred bucks. That's what urban cachet costs these days.

He came around as the girl got out. She was draped in a baggy white shirt, and was skinny as a candle. These two snapped together like magnets and went into lip lock, grinding it out for at least a minute.

I captured the tender scene on my phone. I was able to get the license plate, too.

Finally, they came up for air and the girl ran toward the house. The guy got back in the car, revved up and peeled out.

I got out and walked to the front door. A big, expensive door. Meaning that a camera—yep, there it was—would be trained on whoever approached. I took one of Ira's cards out of my wallet and held it up to the camera, and rang the bell.

A moment later a voice came through the speaker above the doorbell. "Yes?"

"Bianca Aiken?"

"Who are you?"

"I'm an investigator. I work for the lawyer representing Clint."

"What about Clint?"

"He's in jail."

"What?"

"Can we talk?"

Pause. "I don't think so."

"It won't take long."

"I don't want to."

"Bianca, do you know what a subpoena is?"

"A what?"

"A document that compels you to come to court, or get held in contempt. Or even go to jail." A little flair there. "But I don't want that. I just want to ask a couple of questions and then I'll go away."

No response.

"Bianca?"

"Back away."

"Excuse me?"

"Away from the door."

I took a couple of steps backward.

"To the lawn," the voice said.

Whatever. I went to the lawn. A moment later the door opened and Bianca Aiken stepped out. She had one of those faces you would never notice in a crowd. With no makeup and in that floppy shirt, she didn't look like someone who cared if she was noticed or not.

She was holding something in her outstretched hand.

"Pepper spray," she said.

I put my hands up. "You won't need that. Is your mom home?"

"She lives in Texas," Bianca said. "But my dad'll be here soon, so you better go."

"I won't be long, Bianca. I promise."

She gave me an uncertain look. "Why is Clint in jail?"

"He's being charged with possession for sale."

Bianca closed her eyes and shook her head. At least she let her weapon of choice drop to her side.

"How long has Clint been into that?" I said.

"How should I know?"

"You used to be together."

"For like two seconds."

"But you must know him pretty well," I said.

"Not really."

"How about a little?"

She shrugged.

"You go to Elias, right?"

Her eyes flashed. "How do you know that? Who've you been talking to?"

"Bianca, I'm just gathering information."

"Who told you?"

"I keep all my conversations confidential, including this one. Okay?"

She thought about it a moment. "Fine."

"When you two were together, was Clint doing drugs?"

"Just pot," she said.

"He sell it?"

"I don't think so."

"Can you think of anybody who was around him, might have been a seller?"

"It's legal. You can get it anywhere."

"Not if you're sixteen," I said. "Who might he have bought from?"

"Could be anybody, I guess."

"That's the way it is now, huh?"

Another shrug.

I said, "I couldn't help but notice you have a boyfriend."

She stiffened. "You were watching?"

"I was just sitting in my car. It was kind of out there in the open."

"That's none of your business!"

I put my hands up. Delicacy was in order. "You're right, Bianca. It's just a habit I have, gathering information for my clients. Here, take this card." I held it out and approached her slowly. She took it. I stepped back. "Clint's in trouble and maybe you can help him. If you think of anything, or anyone, please call. Mr. Rosen, his lawyer, can get hold of me twenty-four seven."

She nodded. Sadly it seemed. Could have been she was genuinely concerned about Clint and wished she could help. Or maybe she did know something and wasn't ready to talk.

A car zoomed into the driveway. A black Escalade. A man got out and slammed the door.

"What is this?" he said.

Bianca said, "Daddy, this man says I have to go to court."

He glared at me. He looked like a guy who could handle himself in a low-level fight if the conditions were right. "Who are you?"

"My name's Mike Romeo. I work for the lawyer representing Clint Cunningham."

"Clint?" Daddy said. "What's he done now?"

"Now?" I said.

"Last time he was here he broke a bottle of really good wine."

"That was an accident, Daddy."

"A two-hundred-dollar accident."

I said, "Clint's been arrested for selling drugs."

"Not surprised," Daddy said.

"Why not, if I may ask?"

"He's a little out there," he said, making a flitting gesture with his hand.

"He is not," Bianca said. "He just doesn't fit in."

Daddy looked at me and said, "You threatening my daughter?"

I shook my head. "All I want is information to help my client. It's always better to get it through cooperation."

He looked down. "What's that say on your arm?"

I held it up. "Vincit Omnia Veritas."

"Latin?"

"Truth conquers all things."

A half-smile full of skepticism crooked his mouth. "Yeah, like anybody believes that."

"There's a few of us left," I said.

"All right," he said. "Bianca, is there anything you can tell him that might be helpful?"

She shook her head.

Daddy gave me a palms up, nothing-to-see-here gesture.

"Maybe I can ask you a question or two," I said.

"Maybe not," Daddy said. "Maybe it's time for you to go."

"This doesn't have to be difficult," I said.

"You got what you came for, which is nothing," he said.

"Think about it, Bianca," I said. "Clint's in real trouble."

"She doesn't have to think about anything," Daddy said.

"Not anything? Is that what they teach at Elias?"

"Get off my property," he said.

I looked at the girl. "Is that the way you want it?"

Before she could answer, Daddy pushed my shoulder. That was a mistake, and he knew it, because he immediately backed away.

"Look," he said, "I don't want any trouble, okay?"

"Trouble is the interest you'll pay by ignoring the truth."

He just looked at me. I get that a lot.

I drove to Ira's.

He runs his law office out of his house in the Los Feliz district. It's like a second home. Heck, my only home, the place I was housed when I first got to L.A., running ahead of the shadows chasing me.

Ira told me the D.A. was going for the max on Clint. Unless he sang, as the cons put it. The primary reason, Ira explained, was because of the drug involved.

"It's a new street drug," Ira said. "Vector Dust. The name comes from some zombie-like creatures that were in some old TV series. Take it, and you get to be a zombie for awhile."

"It's nice to give kids goals," I said.

"It's not to be trifled with," Ira said. "It's from a family of drugs called cathinones, a stimulant from the plant khat, popular in Somalia. But they've added something, a derivative of crystal meth, which intensifies everything. You get really high, you hallucinate, but paranoia is the cost, and screaming out-of-your-head episodes. Kids have been jumping off buildings. A boy of twelve set himself on fire."

I had to pause a moment over that bit of news.

Finally, I said, "Mexican cartel?"

"Don't think so. It's made in America, just like Budweiser."

"Bikers?"

"Could be," Ira said.

"How did a low-level kid like Clint get into this?"

"That's the question. But he won't tell us."

"Any way to stop him from pleading guilty?"

"Technically, he'll need us to consent to the plea," Ira said.

"And if we don't?"

"He could fire us and represent himself."

"But he's just a kid."

Ira said, "If the court determines he's competent to understand what's going on, there's nothing to stop him. Some jailhouse lawyer is going to tell him he has that option, if he hasn't already."

"What about his mother? Doesn't she have a say?"

"You mean parental rights over a minor child? That has gone the way of the Dodo, Michael."

"Ah, yes. And society is so much better for it."

"Now you're lamenting."

"Observing," I said.

"Well, why don't we observe our case as long as we're still attached to it? What have you got?"

I summarized my interviews with Trista Cunningham and Bianca Aiken. Then showed him Clint's notebook. He looked at a few pages.

"The poetry gets darker as we move along in time," I said. "And then we get to this."

I turned to the skull drawing. "TBD. To Be Done or To Be Determined."

Ira shook his head. "That's corporate-speak, not what a troubled sixteen-year-old would write."

"His mom uses those letters, so maybe he picked up on it."

"Maybe."

"And here's his laptop," I said.

"I'll have a look," Ira said.

"Think you can get in?"

He gave me his who-do-you-think-you're-talking-to look.

"Now this." I showed him the phone photo of the Porsche, the one that had dropped Bianca off at her house.

"Give me a few minutes on this one." Ira's background in intelligence makes him adept at finding things in the ether. He started tapping the keyboard. When he does this, it's like Mozart jotting notes. You don't bother Mozart. I wandered over to his bookshelf—which doesn't have a single uninteresting volume in it—closed my eyes and ran my finger across the spines. I stopped on one and looked. It was Longfellow's translation of Dante's *Inferno*.

Perfect. When I was sixteen at Yale, I read the *Divina Commedia* in Italian. It rhymes perfectly in the original, but that's easier in Italian as almost all their words end in vowels. Longfellow made the wise choice in not forcing rhymes while keeping the cadence of the poet.

I started reading.

M*idway upon the journey of life*
  I found myself within a forest dark,
For the straightforward pathway had been lost.

R ight there with you, Dante old sport!
    "Here we go," Ira said.
"Wait a second," I said. "I'm entering hell."

"Not if I can help it," Ira said. "Listen. Car is owned by a Gavin McGuane." Ira did more tapping. "Address in Simi Valley. Ooh, very tony. Gated community."

"Must live with mommy and daddy."

"Let's see what we can find out on social media," Ira said.

"Talk about entering hell."

"Pish. Okay, let's see... Interesting. He's the son of Shane McGuane."

"Is that supposed to mean something?" I said.

"Shane McGuane is the actor. Remember him?"

"No."

Ira looked at the monitor as he scrolled around. "He did that detective show fifteen years ago, *Dolan.*"

"Rings a bell."

"Looks like he's trying for a comeback," Ira said. "Raising money for an indie film. Has a Kickstarter going."

"Anything more about his son?"

"Let's see... Facebook... Instagram... if you want to have a look at this go ahead."

"The sea of narcissism? No thanks."

"Not feeling social, eh?"

"What good does it do? Present company excepted, of course."

Ira put on his rabbinical face—a furrowed brow and concerned expression. "At some point you've got to take risks with other people."

"Oh? Why?"

"It's called living. And loving."

I clapped Dante shut. "Go on."

"Like with Sophie," Ira said.

I shook my head and sat down. "Don't move like that."

"Like what?" Ira said.

"From rabbi to matchmaker."

"What if she is the one, Michael?"

"The one what?"

"The one for you. Everybody needs a one."

"Now you sound like a Hallmark card."

"See?" Ira said. "There you go. Always defensive."

"That's how you keep alive in this world."

"It's not much of a life if you're all alone."

"Spare me your Talmudic chatter," I said, more biting than I meant it to be.

But Ira, bless him, let it slide off his back.

"By the way, I got a call from LAPD," he said. "You knocked out a fellow with a book?"

"Oh, that."

"Oh, that?"

"He was holding a knife."

"But with a book?"

"It was handy. It was Harold Bloom."

"Ah. Well at least Bloom finally served a good purpose."

"So what about the LAPD?"

"A detective has some follow-up questions. He'd like you to call him."

Ira handed me one of his own cards. On the back he'd written a phone number and a name, Detective Coltrane Smith.

"I'll give him a call when I get good and ready," I said.

"Michael."

"And you're not finished yet," I said. "I've got another puzzle for you."

"You sound like an Oompa Loompa," Ira said.

"You're going Willy Wonka on me?"

"Why not?"

"Then find me Brian Cunningham. He has a company called Cunningham Drywall. Think you can locate a build site where he might be working?"

"Does Willy Wonka like chocolate?" Ira said.

"I'll be out back with Dante," I said.

I went out to Ira's backyard. When I first got to L.A. this was my Eden, my garden spot, my little piece of peace in the world. There's a tree in the middle of the yard, with a padded bench underneath the glossy leaves and elegant white flowers of the *magnolia grandiflora.*

I called Detective Smith and left a voicemail, then stretched out on the bench and opened Dante's epic poem. I got to Canto III and the gates of hell. *Through me you pass into the city of woe: Through me you pass into eternal pain... All hope abandon ye who enter here.* That'd make a nice sign on the 101 as you roll into L.A. County.

Before I could get deeper into the abyss, Detective Smith called me back.

"Good time to talk?" he said.

"Perfect. I was about to descend into hell."

Pause. "O-kay. Just wanted to follow up with you on the incident yesterday."

"You mean the attack?"

"Actually, you stopped it before it became an attack. Technically, the only attack came from you."

"That's my rule," I said.

"You have a rule?"

"Five, actually. This was just one of them."

"I guess I should ask what that rule is, seeing as how I'm investigating this thing."

"Yes you should," I said. "My rule is, Do it to them before they do it to you. Or to somebody else."

Pause. "You have an unorthodox manner."

"This I have been told."

"There are a few things you need to know," Smith said.

"The guy you took down is Sammie Sand. He is from a less than desirable family. The Sands have been known to try intimidation against witnesses."

"In what way?"

"Well, a couple of months ago Sammie's older brother, Brock, was up on a battery charge. He slapped around a young woman named Rowena. He didn't like the way she looked at him in a store, so he waited for her and followed her to her car and gave her a couple with the back of his hand. No witnesses, but Rowena was ready to testify. But at jury selection Sammie and his oldest brother, Adam—"

"How many of these Sand fleas are crawling around?"

"Four, including the father."

"He must be a great dad," I said.

"Oh yeah. Did a dime at Pelican Bay."

"The future of America is in good hands."

Detective Coltrane Smith got back to business. "So Sammie and Adam came to jury selection and sat there glaring at Rowena on the other side of the courtroom. Next thing you know she's telling the deputy D.A. she's not going to testify, and if they make her take the stand she'll lie. A case like this depends on the victim's testimony."

"Sure."

"We did all we could to convince her we'd protect her, but she didn't buy any of it. The case gets tossed. Only later did we learn that Sammie made a W sign with his fingers and touched his crotch. That's what Rowena saw."

"Meaning?"

"She has a younger sister named Wanda. Sammie was telling her what the Sand boys were going to do to Wanda."

"So there's your proof," I said. "What more do you need?"

"A witness," Smith said. "Only Rowena saw the gesture."

My head was starting to buzz. "So these lowlifes get away with everything?"

"We'll get Sammie on something. But I wanted to give you a heads-up about these guys."

"How about I give them a heads-up about me?"

"Excuse me?"

"Put me in a cell with Sammie and leave us alone for half an hour."

"I don't think that would look good to the D.A."

"Does any law look good to the D.A.?"

"Not going there, Mr. Romeo."

"Wait a second," I said. "The case against that other Sand brother, the one with Rowena."

"Right. Brock Sand."

"You said the case got tossed."

"Yep."

"Then why would Sammie go after Wanda anyway?"

"Slash and run," Smith said.

"How's that?"

"It's a white supremacist thing. Slash the face of a black girl, then get away. Proves you have the juice, as they say."

"Still doesn't make sense to me," I said. "Sammie'd have to know it'd be easy to connect him to Wanda."

"It may be he wants to go into the joint."

"Proving his juice?" I said.

"That, and smuggling drugs in via his rectal canal."

"Now there's a fun search."

After the call I dropped back into hell with Dante and Virgil. I kept wondering what circle people like the Sands should be in. I wondered if it came down to it, I'd be speeding their arrival.

Ira called to me. "I've got that info you wanted. Who's your Willy Wonka, son?"

It was getting late, but I chanced it anyway. There was a new build on Dixie Canyon Avenue, south of Ventura, in Encino. It's the one Ira flagged after finding work-site permits cross-referencing subcontractors, one of which was *Cunningham Drywall.*

The house was in the latter stages of construction. The exterior was yet to be painted and there were plastic sheets taped over the glassless windows. The front door was open and I could see a couple of guys in coveralls were inside. From this I deduced that Brian Cunningham was somewhere on the premises. It helped that a big, black pickup in the driveway had *Cunningham Drywall* stenciled on the door. I'm sharp that way.

I stepped up to the open door and knocked on the frame. The two workers shot me a look. One of them was standing on a stepladder. The other one, stockier, had his hand on the wall, as if he were pushing it in place.

"Brian Cunningham?" I said.

The stocky guy said, "Yeah?"

"My name's Mike Romeo. I work for the lawyer representing your son."

He paused a moment, then looked back to his work. "What for?"

"You haven't heard?"

"Nope." To the other guy he said, "Go ahead and tape it." The guy took out a roll of tape and started to apply a strip.

"Would you like to hear about it?" I said.

"Nope."

I waited until they finished the tape job, putting on my

best I'm-not-leaving-until-we-talk look. It must have worked because Brian Cunningham came over to me, wiping his hands on the front of his coveralls.

"All right," he said. "What's it about?"

"Clint's in juvi."

"On what charge?"

"Possession for sale."

"Great. Fantastic." He cursed and pulled out a pack of cigarettes. I waited while he lit up and blew a plume of smoke into the Los Angeles air.

He said, "You have a kid, you think he could be something. You'll teach him to play baseball and maybe he'll have an arm and make it to the pros. Or maybe he'll work with you and take over your business someday."

"He's only sixteen," I said. "There's still time."

He took a drag on his cig. "What do you want from me?"

"Is there anything you might know about any of Clint's friends or acquaintances that might be a clue about what he's into?"

"Nope." He thought a moment. "I think he has a girlfriend."

"Had," I said.

"Messed that up too?"

"You think he messes up?"

"Last few years, yes."

I wanted to say, *Have you been there for him? Have you acted like a father? Have you tried to work with who he is instead of who you want him to be?*

But since I knew the answers were all no, I said, "Maybe you should arrange to see him."

"Why?"

"You have to ask?"

He frowned and gave his cigarette another pull. "I'm going back to work now."

I handed him one of Ira's cards. "If anything occurs to you, please give us a call."

He shrugged, put the card in his pocket, flipped his cigarette out to the driveway, and walked back inside the house.

I drove down to Ventura Boulevard to get something to eat. My taste buds requested a pastrami on rye. That brought to mind Jerry's Famous Deli, a Valley eatery for over forty years. But following right behind that thought was another—that Jerry's was out of business, another victim of lockdown liquidation. So it's not even open for take out. It has itself been taken out.

I didn't grow up here, but when you come to stay in L.A. it adopts you. It's a wild crazy aunt of a town, dressed up in boas and bangles and laughing too loud, sometimes getting angry for no apparent reason and throwing a screaming fit, only to calm down and pull you in for a forgiving embrace even though you haven't done anything to be forgiven for. But you forget about that because she's taken you in and shown you good times, the best times of your life. She takes you to the beach at sundown to listen to the waves, to the hills of Hollywood to look down at Dreamtown, to Melrose to eat, to the Valley to stretch out, to downtown where the old buildings offer a friendly how-do-you-do.

And then one day you wake up and she's gone. Without a note. You listen for the laughter and it isn't there. You wonder if she's dead. You wonder if there'll be a resurrection, and if there is will she be Zombie town, with sagging flesh and lifeless eyes? Will she care about you again? Will she even remember you?

Questions unanswered. I settled for driving through an In-N-Out, about the only place worth driving through in this town, and ate my Double-Double in the car on the way home, with extra sauce but no joy.

W hen I got home I left the sliding glass door open so I could hear the ocean through the screen. I opened a bottle of Corona, cut a lime wedge and shoved the wedge into the bottle. I sat at the kitchenette table where I had a fresh notebook and pen waiting. I opened to the first page of the notebook and began writing my chrono-log for Ira. This is a chronological record of my interviews, three so far—Trista Cunningham, Bianca Aiken (for what it was worth, with a side note on her dad), and Brian Cunningham.

When I finished my summaries I turned to a blank page and wrote *Gavin McGuane* at the top of the page. The kid with the fancy car who'd dropped off Bianca at her house and engaged in a little tongue music. There was something odd about that picture. I needed to talk to him for sure. I jotted his actor-father's name in the margin—*Shane McGuane*—more for completeness than anything else. I didn't think I'd need to track him down, unless there was something about his bairn that didn't seem quite right.

On the last page of the notebook I drew what Joey Feint used to call a "name wheel." You set the notebook lengthwise and jot the names of the people you've interviewed in a kind of circle on the page. If any connections besides blood relation come up between names, you draw a line between them. I drew a line from Gavin McGuane to Bianca Aiken and wrote *Boyfriend?* on the line.

I closed the notebook and put the empty Corona bottle in my recycle container. I did some push-ups then stretched out on the sofa with a copy of *The Long Goodbye*. For relaxation, there's nothing like Raymond Chandler. I got lost in the book until I started to fall asleep. I pulled the sofa blanket over me and read another page before nodding off.

I had a dream. It had something to do with dark hallways and closed doors. There were people behind the doors. I could hear them talking but couldn't make out what they were saying. I knocked on one of the doors. No answer. I knocked again.

Only the knock was coming at my door and woke me up.

A guy in a suit was outside my screen door.

"Mr. Romeo?" he said.

"Huh?" I was a little groggy. What time was it? Had to be pretty early in the morning. There was gray light outside, the kind where the sun is fighting to get through fog.

"May I have a word?" the man said.

"Pick one."

"Can we talk?"

"That's three."

I swung my legs over and sat up. *The Long Goodbye* was on the floor where it had fallen during the night.

"Who are you?" I said.

"May I come in?"

"No."

"All right, this is fine. You're an investigator for Ira Rosen on the Cunningham matter."

I got up and walked to the screen. I was still dressed in yesterday's jeans and Hawaiian shirt. The guy—who was around forty and on the short side—certainly knew how to dress. His suit was gray. A crimson pocket handkerchief matched his crimson tie.

"Who wants to know?" I said

"We're both professionals here. Let's proceed that way."

I rubbed my eyes. "Okay, talk."

"On the Cunningham matter—"

"What's your interest?"

"Our interests," he said. "Yours, the boy's, Mr. Rosen's. Naturally, we all want to see this case resolved as quickly and equitably as possible."

"Uh-huh. And it's also the best interest of whoever you're representing. Now who would that be?"

"Let's not make this complicated."

"I like complicated. Keeps me limber."

"Truly, this is not the way to go. All I'm saying is, you can stop your investigation. There's no need. The young man wants to plead guilty and get on with his life."

"How do you know?"

"As I said."

"You haven't said anything."

"Mr. Romeo, this is a friendly visit. Please have a talk with Mr. Rosen and let the matter go."

I slid the screen door open and stepped outside. "Now you're going to tell me who you are."

He gestured with his head that I should look to the left. I did. And saw on my driveway about six-feet-eight inches of well-muscled meanness. He was leaning on the hood of a black sedan, his arms folded across his big chest. He had a bald head, neck tats, and a well-practiced squint.

"Am I supposed to be intimidated?" I said.

"I would be," the guy said.

I grabbed a handful of the guy's coat and dragged him off the steps and to the driveway. The bald guy unfolded his arms like he was getting ready to jump me.

"Hold it," I said, and let go of the guy in the suit. "You don't want to do this. It's not civil."

"You're being unreasonable," the suit said.

"You threaten me with Gargantua and say *I'm* being unreasonable?"

"Step aside," Gargantua said. I wasn't sure if he was talking to his boss or me.

Then the boss stepped aside.

I put my hands up. "Now wait, we can talk this thing over."

"We already have," the boss said.

"I'm not referencing your attempt to get me off the Clint Cunningham matter. I'm talking about the health and welfare of Gargantua here. See, you're on my property, and without invitation, and that makes me surly. When I'm surly, I tend to hurt people. And when I'm awakened from a nice sleep, I get extra surly, and hurt people even more. I'm liable to do permanent damage to this man, and I hate doing that to people. Most of the time, that is."

A dismissive snort issued from Gargantua's nose.

I said, "You have a chance right now to reevaluate your life. You don't have to do this. You could go back and finish middle school."

He told me to shut the eff up.

"Maybe school isn't your calling," I said. "You could pursue a trade."

"Go on," the boss said to his large charge.

Back in the 1890s there was an English boxer by the name of Bob Fitzsimmons. A lightweight by poundage, he stepped up to take on the heavyweight champ, "Gentleman" Jim Corbett. Asked before the fight about the disparity in size, Fitzsimmons remarked, "The bigger they are, the harder they fall."

This is what I was thinking as Gargantua came toward me. His fists were the size of canned hams. One of those landing full force would send me to the hospital. He didn't move like a martial artist—he was heavy-footed and too erect. He was clearly a guy who depended on his size and those meaty mitts.

"One thing," I said. "If you fall in my petunias I'm going to get very angry." I had a nice little flower garden going. There was a twelve-inch marble statuette of Poseidon in the middle of it, keeping watch.

Gargantua lunged at me with a right cross.

I ducked it. His momentum spun him forty-five degrees. I hit him as hard as I could in the kidney area. My fist bounced off solid muscle.

He tried to elbow my face, a good move from him. But I've been in that situation before, in the cage, and instinct pulled my head back.

His deadly, pointy bone whizzed past my nose.

Now we were facing each other again.

He tried a kick next. He wore work boots that were sure to have steel toes.

I, on the other hand, was in my bare feet.

Fortunately, his boot didn't find purchase in my most vulnerable area. But it got my thigh, sending a burn up my spine. Then his big right fist whipped toward me. I ducked but didn't dodge it completely. He got me on the upper side of my head. It was enough to set off fire alarms and have me stumbling to my right.

I fell into my petunias.

This made me mad. Petunias have a shallow root system. Most of their roots stay in the top four to six inches of soil, making them susceptible to water stress. But that's nothing like the stress of a 6'4", 230-pound former cage fighter thudding on top of their delicate pink heads.

And now a big boot was about to smash my face.

I'm a good roller. You have to be in the cage. And you have to be able to roll and get to your feet, fast.

I did that, and grabbed the statuette of Poseidon on the

way up. It has a solid, square base. To confuse my opponent I did a 360 spin, like an Olympic hammer thrower. In this case the hammer was Poseidon. The side of Gargantua's head was the target.

I caught him flush. I couldn't tell if the cracking sound was his head or the statue, but when he went down like a felled redwood, I knew. And I had to wonder if he was dead.

As I gazed at the giant in my petunias, I heard a car door slam. The guy in the suit fired up the sedan, squealed out of my driveway, and tore up Paradise Cove Road, toward PCH.

The side of Gargantua's face was turning an ugly purple. I knelt and felt for his pulse. It was thrumming, slowly.

Now what? Not having a hydraulic lift handy, I took hold of his thick wrists and dragged him out of my flower garden.

It was like hauling a full refrigerator, but I managed to get him to the nook in the back of my mobile home, where the pipes for my water hookup stick out of the concrete. I went inside and got a pair of steel handcuffs. I cuffed his right wrist to the pipes. Had the guy been at his best I would have worried he'd rip the pipes right out. But he wasn't going to be doing any ripping any time soon.

I went in again and started the coffee maker. I got *The Long Goodbye* and went back out and sat on the steps to read. Gargantua was breathing steadily. When the coffee maker beeped I got myself a cup and came back out and was met with the befuddled look of a wounded grizzly.

"What'd you do?" Gargantua said. He touched the side of his face with his left hand, and winced.

"You were smote by the god of the sea," I said.

"Whu?"

"Had to do it. It was you or me."

"What are you gonna do now?"

"How about a little friendly conversation?" I said.

He blinked a couple of times. "I don't get you."

"Not many people do. Sometimes I don't even get myself."

He got a frustrated look on his puffy face. "Just tell me what you want and get this over with."

I said, "You're obviously freelance. Who's the guy who so shamelessly ran out on you?"

"That was part of the deal."

"What was?"

"If I got messed up instead of messing you up. No guarantees."

"It was still rather uncivil for your ride to take off."

He squinted. "You talk weird."

"So what was this guy's name?"

"I can't tell you," he said.

"Can't, or won't?"

"Does it matter?"

"It matters whether I use persuasion or coercion."

"Hurry up and do what you're gonna do."

"Quit sounding so fatalistic," I said. "You have human agency. You have the power of choice."

"Man, will you just talk plain?"

"What part of human agency don't you understand?"

"Cut it out!"

I leaned back for a moment and let him stew in uncertainty. Interrogation 101.

Finally, I said, "What's your name?"

He hesitated, calculating his option. Then said, "Nick."

"Let's be sensible, Nick. I don't want to hurt you

anymore. And you don't want to hurt me. Your employment effectively ended when your employer drove away. Why not give me his name so I can find him and, you know, give him a piece of my mind?"

"Don't know his name."

"He pay you?"

Silence.

"Work with me, Nick. The sooner you do the sooner you get out."

"I got five hundred up front," he said. "Supposed to get another five if I..."

"Beat me up?"

"Only if I had to," he said.

"Didn't quite work out," I said. "But you should at least get something for a good faith effort."

"Yeah, right."

"You ever work for that guy before?"

He shook his head.

"How'd you get the job?"

"Guy I knew in the slam does a lot of work for him. Asked me if I wanted in."

"This friend—"

"Not a friend. Just a guy I knew."

"He hooked you up with the guy who drove you out here?"

Nick nodded.

"Where'd you meet up with this guy?" I said.

"He picked me up at a McDonald's in Reseda."

"You do this kind of thing regularly?" I asked.

"No, man," Nick said. "I needed the money."

"Out of a job?"

"Where is there any work in this town for a guy like me?"

"Maybe your fr—the guy you were in the joint with—

maybe he could tell us where to find the guy who drove you here."

"No way. More likely he won't want to talk to me ever again."

"Let's see what I can do."

"What do you mean?"

"I can be persuasive."

Nick winced and tenderly touched his face. "I know."

I went inside and got some ice and put it in a plastic bag. I came back out with the ice and a butterfly knife.

"I don't know you well enough to trust you yet," I said. "But I'm willing to take the next step. I'll hand you this ice bag for your face, but if you try anything, I'll gut you like a fish. Is that fair?"

"More than fair, man," he said. "I don't want any part of you."

I gave him the bag. He put it on the side of his face that Poseidon had so imperiously mashed.

"What were you in the joint for?" I asked.

"Voluntary manslaughter," he said.

"Tell me about it."

"Why?"

"It'll redeem our time."

"Do what?"

"Omnia tempus revelat."

He frowned, and it looked like it hurt.

"Sorry, chum," I said. "Quotes tend to pop into my mind. It means 'Time reveals all.' So tell me about the manslaughter."

He paused a moment, then said, "Drug deal gone bad. I was muscle for a crazy parolee I knew, and had to thump a kid who drew a knife." He paused again. "I didn't want him to die. They were gonna hang a murder charge on me and El-Wop."

By which he meant LWOP—Life Without Parole.

He went on. "I got a young public defender who fought like a young public defender, not an old, tired one. My co-defendant got the max, but the jury hung on my charge. The D.A. didn't want another trial and offered me the VM. I took it. I deserved it."

"But you were ready to thump me."

"I know what I can do," Nick said. "I wouldn't have killed you."

"That's very comforting."

"No hard feelings?"

"Let's leave feelings out of it," I said. "Most of the world's woes have been caused by feelings overcoming rationality."

"There you go again with that talk. Why are you like this?"

"Great question," I said.

His eyes got glassy. "I think I'm gonna hurl."

I backed away quick, as a hurling from a man this size covers a lot of ground. "Take some nice, easy breaths," I said.

He tried to. "I'm dizzy."

"Let me take you to a doctor."

"No way!"

"Relax. She's a friend. She lives here."

"Just lemme go."

"You're coming with me. Remember the knife." I held it up. "I'm going to unlock you and see if you can stand."

. . .

Artra Murray lives in a unit about a hundred yards from mine. She's middle-aged and a doctor. A great doctor. The first African American woman to become head of surgery at Johns Hopkins. After a few years there she went to Kenya as a missionary surgeon. She now runs a health clinic up near Pepperdine University.

I walked the unsteady Nick to her place and knocked on the door.

Artra answered. She was in her bathrobe, holding a cup of coffee. "Mike, what's up—" She gave Nick a look. "Hoo boy."

"Can you have a look at him?" I said.

"Bring him in."

We went inside.

"Sit him down there," Artra said, pointing to her futon.

I helped Nick to the futon. He was still holding the ice bag to his face. Artra took it from him and handed it to me. Then she leaned over and looked at the purple side of his face.

"Okay," she said. "What happened?"

"We had a little scuffle," I said.

Nick said, "Puhh."

"You hit him?" Artra said.

"With a marble statuette," I said.

She stood up and looked at me. Not approvingly.

"It's a long story," I said.

"*You're* a long story," she said. "Is the trouble over now?"

"Yes," I said.

"Then put that knife away."

I put it in my pocket.

Artra went back to Nick. "How you feeling?"

"Not good," Nick said.

"Dizzy?"

"Yeah."

"I'm going to ask you to do something for me. Look straight ahead... That's it." She held her hand out about two inches from the left side—the purple side—of his face. "Just with your eyes, look at my hand."

He tried. His eyes looked jerky to me.

She repeated this with the other side of his face.

"Do you know where you are?" Artra said.

"Your place," Nick said.

"And what part of town is my place located?"

He blinked a couple of times. "I don't know."

She leaned in a little closer. "Considering what you used on him, *Mister* Romeo, there's a good chance we have a zygomaticomaxillary fracture. Broken cheekbone. I'm going to want to take a closer look. Can you get him to the clinic?"

"I don't wanna go to no clinic," Nick said.

"Young man," Artra said, "you could have a major problem. An injury like this can affect your eating, even your breathing. You could even need surgery."

"No surgery!" Nick said.

"Easy, big fella," I said.

"Lemme out of here," Nick said.

"I strongly advise against that," Artra said.

"I wanna go home," Nick said.

Artra put her hands on her hips. "You're acting like a child. You're too big to act like a child. Way too big."

"No hospital," Nick said.

"It's a clinic," Artra said. "It won't take long to—"

"No clinic," Nick said.

Artra shook her head and looked at me. "I can't make him go. So you're going to have to be responsible for him."

"What?" I said.

"You're the one who hit him."

"He was going to break *my* face."

"Nevertheless," Artra said, "you are going to keep an eye on him and report back to me. Understand?"

"For how long?" I said.

"The rest of the day, at least. Call me in a few hours." She looked at Nick. "I'll give you something for the pain. But you need to work with Mike, okay?"

"I just wanna go home," Nick said.

"That's not the answer I was looking for," Artra said. "Work with Mike."

"Okay, okay," Nick said. "Can I go home now?"

Nick barely fit in Spinoza. But with the top down and the fresh air blowing, he seemed okay with it. As we started up Topanga Canyon, I said, "What did you do when you got out of the joint?"

"I got a job washing dishes at a restaurant in Sherman Oaks. Nice couple owned the place. Spent all this money putting in Plexiglas and doing what they were told so they could open up, remember that?"

"Unfortunately," I said.

"So they do, and then the mayor closes 'em down again. They lost the place. The wife killed herself."

"Collateral damage."

"What?"

"Casualty in a war that's been bungled from the start," I said.

"I got mad when it happened," Nick said. "Kinda crazy mad. That's when I started doing some hurt work."

"Through your parolee guy."

"Uh-huh."

"Who I'm going to talk to," I said.

"That's not a good idea, man."

"I'll try to work it out."

"I seen the way you work," Nick said. "San works that way, too."

"San?"

"San Dae-Ho. That's his name."

"Sounds Korean."

"I don't know any of that stuff."

"What can you tell me about him?"

"That he's bad."

"I've dealt with that before," I said.

"He's not tall, maybe five-eight or nine. But he's ripped. He's into some kind of martial arts."

"Yeah? Which ones?"

"Tackado, something like that."

"Taekwando?"

"Yeah, I think that's it. You into that stuff?"

"I was," I said.

"Not anymore?"

"Only when I need to be."

Nick snorted. "Like when you got a statue in your hand?"

"No, Nick. That was the ancient art of grabbo."

"The what?"

"Grab whatever you can to smash a guy before he puts a boot on your face."

I caught a glimpse of Nick smiling.

"So where can I find this San Dae-Ho?" I said.

"I don't know. I only met him a couple of times on the outside, in places he picked."

"But he's some sort of contact for freelance enforcers?"

"I guess so. I'd stay away from him if I was you."

"Into the valley of death rode the six hundred," I said.

"Man, why do you talk funny?"

"Funny?"

"Yeah, what you just said, and philosophers and Latin and all that."

"I did some time in college," I said.

"Where?"

"Yale."

"Seriously?"

"I was serious about it at the time."

"So why aren't you a lawyer or something?" he said.

"Why aren't you an Eagle Scout?" I said.

"Huh?"

"Things happen out of our control. With domineering hand Fortune moves the turning wheel."

"There you go again!"

"It's from a guy named Boethius," I said. "He wrote it when he was in the joint."

"He was in the joint?"

"In Northern Italy, around 523 A.D."

Nick shook his head.

I said, "So what he meant was that things move, out of our control, and all we can do is respond. A guy dies, and you go to prison. How do you respond? My parents die, and I..."

A pause lingered, then Nick said, "Your parents are dead?"

"Yeah."

"But you're not that old."

"The wheel turns."

We didn't speak for awhile after that. At the top of Topanga you could look down at the Valley. It was clear that day. You could see the green hills dotted with expensive homes, down to the valley floor and the jut of tinted glass buildings in Warner Center, all the way across to the Santa Susana mountains. From here the Valley actually looked inviting—placid, sunny, the kind of place that drew swarms of returning soldiers after World War II, buying tract houses on the GI Bill and stuffing them with wives and kids. There were jobs, too, from the local filling station to the burgeoning aerospace industry. Chicken ranches and orchards gave way to shopping centers and industrial parks. The public school system was actually good in those days, as in, they actually educated the kids and enforced self-control in the classrooms.

But drop down into the mournful details of lockdown L.A., and you got the feeling the place had been gutted. The sense of optimism sucked out. Big industry is no more, and public education has had a long, slow, painful decline. The Valley was about survival now, without the beauty and insouciance of former times.

Reseda is one of the older neighborhoods, with the old homes to show for it. Nick lived in the garage of one of those homes. It was on Hemmingway (two Ms) Street. It was a scruffy looking house, dirty beige with a flat roof. It desperately needed some care. The lawn was patchy, the asphalt driveway cracked, and the front window had white plaster patching around it. At the side of the house was a wooden gate, the bottom of which was warped by water damage. Whoever said it never rains in Southern California was probably on mushrooms when he wrote that.

Through the gate was the garage where Nick was living. He told me the guy who was renting the house was the nephew of the owner, and both of them were ex-cons who knew how to cut breaks for their fellows. The space was pretty drab. A mattress with a couple of blankets, a little refrigerator, a Coleman stove, a small TV, and boxes with clothes spilling out of them. I told Nick to lie down and rest. He didn't fight me on that. He spread out on the mattress like a beached whale.

"I'm going to step outside and make a call," I said.

"You don't have to stay," Nick said.

"I promised Dr. Murray."

"I'll be okay."

"Be right back."

I went out to the driveway and called Ira. "I got a visit this morning. At the Cove. Some joker telling us to back off of the Cunningham case."

"Joker?" Ira said.

"Nattily dressed. He had muscle with him."

"Uh-oh."

"Yeah. I had to take him out."

"Michael…"

"No worries. I'm here with him now."

"The joker?"

"The muscle."

Pause. "Please explain yourself."

"He's a rather large fellow. We had a fight in my petunia garden. You know how I love my petunias."

"Get to the point, please."

"I had to bash him in the face with my Poseidon statuette."

Nothing from Ira. I could imagine him rubbing the bridge of his nose.

I said, "As that was going on, the joker took off, leaving his hired thug in my care."

"*Care* did you say?"

"We talked it out," I said. "I had Artra take a look at him."

"Wait a second. You took your latest victim to see Artra? And he went?"

"Life is funny that way," I said. "Then I brought him home. I'm in Reseda. What I'm trying to find out is who that joker is. Nick—that's the muscle—doesn't know. He only knows he was hired for this job by a guy named San Dae-Ho. I'll need to talk to him."

"Talk?"

"An expansive definition of talk I'll admit."

"Michael, when you get this way—"

"I'll be charming," I said.

"Just hold off. I got a call from the court. Clint is moving to go pro se. There's a hearing on Thursday. We may be off this case."

"You may be," I said.

"Michael..."

"I don't like people showing up at my house and messing up my flowers," I said.

"There is a Jewish saying, Michael. May God protect you from bad people and save you from yourself."

"Ira?"

"Yes?"

"I'm not Jewish."

"More's the pity," Ira said.

I went back inside the garage. Nick was staring at the ceiling.

"How you feeling?" I said.

"Bad."

"Headache?"

"More of a face ache."

"Does it hurt when you laugh?"

"Huh?"

"Give me your phone number. I'll check with you later."

"You going?"

"Problem?"

"I dunno," he said. "I don't know what's going on anymore."

I squatted next to him. "You've had a shock to the system. You need rest. Just take the next couple of days and do as little as possible. Take aspirin for the head."

"Like I've got anything else to do."

"How about reading a book?"

"What?"

"A book. You know, with pages and a cover."

"I don't like to read."

"Maybe we can change that," I said.

"Whatever."

"You just relax now, okay?"

"Whatever."

"And stop saying that. That's a word for losers."

"Yeah? Look at me."

"Nil desperandum," I said.

Nick groaned.

"Never say die," I said.

I drove over to Jimmy Sarducci's gym. Jimmy is a short, talkative fight trainer who runs a nice boxing and MMA facility. He lets me work out there for nothing, in part because I helped him in the past, and in part because he wants to put me back in the cage. He thinks he can make me a star. I need that publicity like I need an extra belly button.

I parked on the street because the parking lot behind the gym was covered with a canopy. At the height of the L.A. lockdowns Jimmy had been forced outside to his parking lot. He was keeping it there, not trusting a city that said to restaurants *You can open. Oops, no you can't. Sorry you spent all that money on prep...* There was a mat and a rope ring around it for sparring, a heavy bag, a couple of punching dummies, and a weight station.

Jimmy was sitting on a stool watching a couple of guys sparring in the ring.

"Hey, Mike!" Jimmy said when he saw me coming.

He held out his fist.

"Really?" I said.

"We gotta do what we gotta do."

"Jimmy," I said, "if masculine grips are outlawed, only outlaws will have masculine grips."

He thought about it for a second, then opened his hand. We shook.

I looked at the ring. "Contenders?"

"Tomato cans," Jimmy said. "Maybe I can turn 'em into pugs."

"It's good to have a goal."

"You here to work out?" Jimmy said.

"I'm here with a question."

Jimmy looked at his fighters. "Stick and move! Stick and move!"

I said, "I'm trying to locate a martial arts guy by the name of San Dae-Ho."

"What kind of name is that?"

"Probably Korean. He's about five-eight, jacked. Anybody like that come around?"

"Not here."

"Maybe you could make a call or two to some of your contacts," I said. "Guy like that is sure to stick out somewhere."

"Do I look like an information service to you?" Jimmy said.

"Whoa," I said.

"Ah, I'm just grumpy about everything. Open, not open,

open again, but you gotta wear this, stay away from that. I'll make some calls."

"You're a prince," I said.

Jimmy uttered an Italian phrase that sounded like a curse or a dinner order. Then, "When you gonna get in the cage again? You're wasting your prime. We could make some real money, you and me."

"Haven't you heard? Love of money is the root of all kinds of evil."

Jimmy cursed—or ordered food—again.

I took my leave.

I drove out to Simi Valley to see if I could catch Gavin McGuane at home.

Simi Valley, unlike its much bigger cousin to the east, is a bedroom community known for its placid pace and relatively safe existence. It has its own police department, but a lot of L.A. cops live there, too. Controlled growth keeps the sprawl contained.

The McGuane house was on a winding street where homes approaching mansion size dotted a hilly landscape. The house was Mediterranean in style with a fancy stone exterior and long driveway leading up to a three-car garage. A medium-sized liquidambar tree was the showpiece of the front yard. Almost barren of leaves at this time of year, in the fall its shiny, maple-like leaves would bring an explosion of vibrant red and orange. Two points for whoever designed the yard.

There was one car in the driveway, a metallic-blue BMW Alpina sedan. As I walked by the car I glanced in the passenger-side window. On the seat were some flyers. They had a picture of a beautiful home with a large SOLD banner across the top. On the left side of the flyer was a woman.

She was model-gorgeous, posed with arms folded and a confident smile. Below the picture was printed *Mandi McGuane. Call Mandi and Start Packing!* At the bottom of the flyer was the logo for Keller Williams Realty.

I rang the bell at the front door. A moment later a Hispanic woman opened the door and waited for me to say something. I'd come to talk to Gavin, but switched my intro to, "May I speak with Mandi McGuane, please?"

The woman gave me a quick scan dripping with uncertainty. I couldn't blame her. I handed her one of Ira's cards and said, "This concerns Gavin."

She frowned, then said, "Please wait," and closed the door.

I whistled a merry tune and looked out at the view. I could see a good portion of Simi Valley. They used to shoot Westerns out here. Now the place is covered with homes and stores and offices. No elbow room anymore for John Wayne or Clint Eastwood. And that means the end of the frontier spirit. We've packed ourselves in on each coast and grown soft and spineless.

The door opened and the woman said, "Follow me, please."

She led me through a massive foyer with a cathedral ceiling, into a formal living room with wood flooring, luxury furniture, ornate fireplace.

"Just one moment," the woman said, and walked out the other side of the living room. I wandered over to a wall of windows looking out at a backyard with a pebble-tech pool and four rock waterfalls.

I heard a scuffing sound. It came from a big cage with a big bird in it. A macaw. Blue-and-gold head, green feathers, hooked black beak, and beady eyes that glared at me with suspicion. I stared right back. No bird was going to make a monkey out of me.

"*That's not going to work for us,*" the macaw said.

Unsure how to respond, I said, "And why not?"

The parrot moved an inch to the right on its standing perch. "*The comps don't support that price.*"

A voice behind me said, "That's Marco."

I turned and saw the woman from the flyer. The photo had not done her justice. She was five-eight or nine, with lustrous tawny hair billowing over her shoulders. She wore a black pencil skirt with matching coat over a white blouse. She had on a jade necklace that was just this side of ostentatious. In one hand she held a smartphone, in the other Ira's card.

She stopped six feet away from me, looked at the card, then back at me. Her sea-green eyes looked like they could laser through a bank safe.

"What's this about?" she said.

"My name is Mike Romeo," I said.

"Who is Ira Rosen?"

"The lawyer I work for."

"What do you want? What's this about Gavin? Is he in some sort of—"

Her phone played a tune. It sounded like the first vibrant notes of David Benoit's "Freedom at Midnight."

"Excuse me, I have to take this," she said. She pressed the phone to her ear and said, "Hello, Sanjay," and walked out of the room. I heard her fading voice say, "No, no, the HOA fee is included... yes, I explained that..."

So I looked around the living room some more. At least she had a bookshelf with actual books in it. More and more homes don't have bookshelves. Game consoles, yes. Wall-mounted TVs, check. But fewer covers with paper pages between them.

"*Lush views from every room,*" Marco said.

I turned to the cage. "I'll give you ten thousand dollars for it."

"*That's not going to work for us.*"

Mandi came back in. "Sorry about that. But I've got five deals going and have to be on call."

"You must do it pretty well."

"I've worked hard to become a top producer," she said.

"The American way."

"I thought so, too. But they want to tax me into oblivion. That's what you get for being successful these days."

"I try to hover just around the poverty line," I said.

She smiled. It was an easy, self-assured smile. At the same time, her eyes changed from polite to interested. She knew how to use those eyes. If they ever got seductive, most men standing where I was would start biting their fists. I kept my hands loose.

She said, "What about Gavin?"

"I'm an investigator for Mr. Rosen. We're representing Clint Cunningham."

She shook her head. "I don't know that name."

"Clint had a girlfriend named Bianca Aiken."

"I don't know that name, either."

"Oh? Because I think Gavin is seeing her."

"I'm not up on everything Gavin does," she said. "You know how it is."

"I'm not sure I do."

"High school boys. Living with their mother. They keep things to themselves."

"Does he go to Elias?" I said.

"How did you know?" she said.

"Clint Cunningham and Bianca both go there."

"You've done homework," she said. "I like that. Information is the key to negotiation."

"I'm not here to negotiate," I said.

"Oh, I don't know. You want me to answer questions. I could tell you to take a flying leap, and you can try to convince me. Everything's negotiation."

"Or compulsion."

She cocked her head.

"Themistocles," I said. "Ancient Greek politician. He said, 'I have two gods—persuasion and compulsion.' "

"Ho-ly cow," Mandi said. "Who on earth are you? Quoting Greeks, for heaven's sake."

"Have I persuaded you to answer a few questions?"

"You have bought yourself a little more time. Have a seat." She sat in one of the plush chairs and crossed her legs like an Egyptian queen. I sat like a Roman senator.

"Go ahead," she said.

"How does Shane figure into Gavin's life?"

"More homework, eh?"

"Shane is a pretty well-known actor."

"Was."

"Maybe will be again."

"Narcissists never believe their time is over."

"I take it you're not on good terms with him."

"He's a child. And he likes to throw tantrums. Ever try to talk to a narcissistic child throwing a tantrum?"

"I'm not on Twitter, so no."

That brought another easy smile to her face.

"But you still go by McGuane," I said.

"I built my brand on that name," she said. "Can't change it now. I've got a dozen bus stop benches around town."

"Sensitive question. Have you ever thought Gavin might be doing drugs?"

If it was sensitive to her, she didn't show it. "No," she said.

"Even with the high-school-boy-keeping-things-from-his-mother bit?"

Her pleasant expression gave way to tight cheek muscles and narrowed eyes. "This is starting to feel like an interrogation," she said.

"It's no news flash that drug use has spiked among kids, what with the lockdowns and all. My case has a drug angle, and I thought maybe Gavin might have something to tell me, seeing as he's with my client's old girlfriend, and they go to the same school. Make sense?"

"A little. But there's nothing I can tell you."

"Maybe you can tell me how Gavin got his car."

"What?"

"Did you buy it for him? His dad?"

"What are you fishing for?"

"It's expensive machinery. Somehow I don't think Gavin is a top producer."

That brought her to her feet. "I think we're finished here."

I stood. "Just doing my job. You're a professional. You can understand that."

She gave me a long, lingering look. Was it the look of a fellow professional, or more like a lion sizing up a zebra? "I'll have a chat with Gavin. If I think there's something you should know, I'll call you."

"If I wanted to chat with Shane, how would I go about it?"

"Ha. Get a cattle prod. He's not the talkative type."

"That's compulsion," I said. "I can try persuasion."

She folded her arms, just like in the flyer. "You know, I think you could. Ever think of going into real estate?"

"Never," I said.

"I could train you."

Visions of me jumping through a hoop flashed into my mind. "Thanks for the offer, but—"

"Just think about it," she said. "Now, as for Shane, he's a

little boy. Be prepared for that. He's not likely to talk to you over the phone. I could tell you where he lives, but he won't open the door for you."

"Any suggestions?"

"He likes to hang out with a group of guys, stuntmen mostly. Makes him feel studlier. I know they've been having lunches at Tab's Hot Dogs in Canoga Park. They have outdoor tables there. Can't tell you when, but it's a shot. You have a picture of him?"

"Only what I've seen on the net."

"Look for him to be wearing shades and a backward baseball cap. I swear, he's eight years old."

She took a silver card holder out of her pocket, opened it, and handed me a card. It had her picture on it and her realtor info.

"Buy or sell," she said.

"Everybody's a potential client, eh?" I said.

"That's how you make it in this business."

"I'll follow up with you in a few days," I said.

"That's not going to work for us," Marco said.

I t was getting toward lunchtime anyway, so I drove back to the Valley and pulled into the shopping plaza where Tab's Hot Dogs was located. It was in the corner, next to a Ross Dress for Less store. There was a lone muncher at an outdoor table.

I went in and ordered an L.A. Street Dog, bacon-wrapped with mayo, mustard, grilled peppers and onions, jalapeños, diced tomatoes. All the finer things in life. I added fries and a Coke to the order, just to make sure I was eating a balanced meal.

Outside, I took a table by the door. There were five other tables, empty except for that one guy. I munched and watched the cars going in and out, and thought about Sophie Montag. I thought about how my life might have been if I'd gone into academia, where I belonged. And what it would have been like to meet Sophie then, and settle in with her and teach at some midwestern college.

But then again, had I stayed back East and pursued a doctorate, I wouldn't have met Ira Rosen, wouldn't have ended up in L.A., and wouldn't have gone to the bookstore where Sophie worked. It's all a game of chance and you don't control the wheel.

But at least there is the hot dog to make wherever we sojourn more bearable.

In the time it took me to down the entirety of my meal, several people had entered the place and left with take out. Only one other person sat down at a table, a young guy in an Amazon delivery vest. He ate like an escaped convict. He had a schedule to keep.

As my stakeout was turning into a bust, I gave Ira a call to update him on my doings. I got his voicemail, which was odd. He always picks up for yours truly. Then I remembered today was the hearing where Clint Cunningham was going to try to get us fired so he could represent himself.

And if that happened, what then? I'd stop questioning witnesses, sure, but there was still a great big question mark hanging out there. I hate hanging question marks. I want to smash them.

I wanted to know who tried to intimidate me off the case. I needed to find that guy who showed up at my place with Nick, and who put him on to me. I did not want anyone coming back to my house and stepping on my petunias.

As I was walking back to my car, a Jeep SUV with tinted windows almost splattered me on its grill. It pulled into a space and four guys got out. They didn't so much as glance my way. They were laughing about something. One of them wore sunglasses and a backward baseball cap. They all wore masks.

They chattered into Tab's. I walked back to the table I'd been sitting at and sat again. The Amazon delivery guy was gone. So when the four of them came out with their dogs and picked the table next to mine, we were the only customers. They were still laughing about something. From the words and gestures, I got the impression it was something about a woman.

The guy in the backward baseball cap was definitely Shane McGuane. Research told me he was 49, which made his cap wearing more than a bit ridiculous. His companions were younger, occupying an age range somewhere between thirty and forty. They had different builds, but each was solid in its own way. Like stuntmen.

I watched them for a few minutes. They had moved their masks to Abe Lincoln chin-beard position. The conversation turned from the unnamed woman to the Lakers. An argument broke out about LeBron, and much cursing ensued. Not exactly a meeting of the Socratic Debating Society.

When there was a space in the talk I said, "Shane McGuane?"

He looked over at me. He gave me one of those chin-up nods that communicates *How you doin'?*

The stuntmen all looked at me with varying degrees of annoyance.

I said to McGuane, "Wonder if I could have a word with you."

He spread his hands and spoke around the food in his mouth. "Having my lunch, bruh."

"It won't take long," I said.

One of the stuntmen, the one with the baldest head,

looked at me and said, "He's having his lunch, didn't you hear?"

"It's about Gavin," I said.

The three stuntmen looked at McGuane, as if awaiting orders. McGuane asked me who the eff I was.

"I work for a lawyer," I said. "There's a—"

"What's she up to now?" McGuane said.

"Who?" I said.

"My ex," he said. "That b—"

"Nothing to do with your ex," I said.

"Then how'd you know to find me here?"

"I did talk to Mandi," I said. "But it was about Gavin."

One of the other stuntmen, who had a noticeable scar on his cheek said, "You want us to show this guy to his car?"

McGuane didn't say anything for a long moment. The three stunts seemed almost vibrating with anticipation.

"I'll give you a minute," McGuane said, getting out of his chair and taking the other one at my table. His friends looked deflated.

"Well?" McGuane said.

"I'm an investigator for a lawyer. We're representing a classmate of Gavin's. He's been arrested on a drug dealing charge. I was hoping to talk to Gavin about all this."

"You think Gavin's involved?"

"I wanted to talk to him because he might have information helpful to our client."

McGuane told me what I was full of.

"That's not helpful," I said.

McGuane gave me a two-word dismissal and returned to his table.

I said, "You do know we can issue a subpoena to you and Gavin both, right?"

McGuane told me where I could shove my subpoena.

At which point the noticeable scar stuntman stood up

and walked over to me and said, "Man wants to eat now."

"Yes," I said, not moving. "A man needs to eat."

"Take off."

"Go on back and enjoy your hot dog. Which one did you get?"

He slapped me.

Now, I am a reasonable man. I will engage with anyone on important matters in a rational, loquacious fashion.

Slaps are another matter. I don't usually talk after a slap to the face. I do think about one of my rules. *Do unto them before they do unto you.* He was definitely looking to do something more unto me.

I shot up out of my chair and gave him a web strike to the throat. That's the webbing between thumb and forefinger, aimed at his thyroid cartilage. It's not as bad as a hard strike to the trachea, which can be lethal. But it's enough to shut a guy up.

Scar grabbed his throat with both hands and dropped to his knees, sucking for air, eyes bulging.

Of course the two other stuntmen had to come to his aid. Which meant after me.

A metal chair makes a nice weapon, but you have to know where to aim it. If you go for an overhand to the head, a smart fighter will duck and charge. The force will be dissipated and you'll have an adrenaline-laced bull taking you down to the ground. If you try for a side swipe, you may land a blow, but if at somebody who's in shape, they'll come at you with a fist from the other side.

But the knees are another story. One good clout to the prayer bones and you can take a guy out for a good long time.

That's what I gave to Bald Guy.

Which left number three, who was lean and mean. The stringy-muscular type. This kind can give you the most trouble. They're wiry and fast and pack more of a punch than you'd suppose just by looking at them.

It had taken me five seconds to dispatch the first two, who were now moaning on the ground. That gave Stringy pause for a second.

But only a second. When he pulled out a knife he looked ready for action.

I was still holding the chair like a lion tamer.

"Put that thing away," I said, "or I'll make you eat this chair."

Stringy tossed the knife to his other hand then back again—an old-school gang move meant to intimidate.

I shook my head. I was already planning my first couple of moves when Shane McGuane piped in.

"Put it away," he said.

"What?" Stringy said.

"Put that knife away. Now!"

After a moment's pause, Stringy slipped the knife back into the side sheath he wore.

"I don't need this kind of publicity," he said, both to me and his boys.

The young woman who worked behind the counter came out to the patio, her eyes wide over her mask. "Oh my God! What's happening?"

Shane McGuane got to his feet. "Nothing."

The woman looked at the two stuntmen who were on the ground, then at me. I was still holding the chair.

"Just moving to another table," I said.

The poor woman didn't know what to do. She stood there, holding the door open with one hand.

"I should call the police," she said.

"No!" Shane McGuane said.

I put the chair down and said, "No need for the police. These gentlemen were just leaving," giving McGuane a nice, firm glare. Now I had leverage over an aging actor trying to make a comeback and fearing he'll show up on TMZ or some viral phone video.

"Come on, come on," McGuane said, helping his friends to their feet. Scar was just starting to get his wind back. Baldy had a noticeable limp. Skinny stared at me the way guys do when they imagine blood spurting out of your neck.

They left their food on the table and shambled toward the Jeep.

The woman looked at me as if asking what she should do.

"It was just an unfortunate misunderstanding," I said. "No real harm done."

"Are you sure?"

"Absolutely."

"They come here a lot," she said.

"I'm sure they'll come again."

"What about you?"

"I like your fare," I said. "I'll be back."

"But maybe not when those guys are here, okay?"

I drove over to Jimmy's to see if he had any info on finding San Dae-Ho. When I got there two guys were fighting in the ring. Not sparring or boxing. Street fighting.

Jimmy was outside the ropes screaming at them to cut it out. When they grappled to the mat, Jimmy climbed through the ropes and tried to separate them. They held together like two pythons trying to choke the life out of each other.

One fighter was white, the other black. Their face

coverings were long gone.

Jimmy was having no luck breaking it up. Black Guy was on top of White Guy, pressing his forearm into White Guy's throat. White Guy had his legs wrapped around Black Guy, but clearly was running out of oxygen.

Jimmy kept screaming.

The pythons kept coiled.

I went in and grabbed Black Guy's forearm so White Guy could breathe.

"Let loose," I said.

Black Guy issued a two-word retort.

White Guy called him the name that shall not be named.

Black Guy went berserk and broke free of my grip. He rammed his elbow into White Guy's face.

I threw a bicep squeeze around Black Guy's neck and pulled, prying him off like a layer of sheet metal from an airplane fuselage. We rolled back and I flipped him, transitioning to a full nelson and complete submission.

He tried to reverse me. Didn't work.

"Cool off now," I said.

He repeated his two words.

Jimmy yelled, "Get outta here! The both o' yuz! I don't want you around here no more!"

"Hold it!" I said. "I don't want these guys going off and killing each other."

I let go of Black Guy and got between him and White Guy, who was sitting up and bleeding from the nose.

"Get him a towel, Jimmy," I said.

White Guy touched his face, looked at the blood on his hand and got up ready to fight.

I said, "Either of you tries anything I'll lay you out until Tuesday."

"I didn't do anything!" Black Guy said. "He started in

with the name calling."

White Guy said, "Snowflake can't take it."

Black Guy started to charge. I pushed him back.

"Let me take him!" Black Guy said.

"Bring it!" White Guy said

"Stop!" I felt like a teacher's assistant on an elementary school playground. "Cool off."

"I want 'em outta here," Jimmy said.

"Go help him clean up," I said, indicating the nose bleeder. To Black Guy I said, "Come talk a minute."

"Nothing to talk about," he said.

"Humor me," I said.

With one more withering glance at his erstwhile opponent, Black Guy came with me to the far corner of the ring.

"What was it all about?" I said.

"You heard it," he said.

"The names?"

"Yeah."

"You know this guy?"

He shook his head. "We just decided to spar. I got in a couple good shots and he starts throwing shade."

"Speaking of names, mine's Mike."

He paused. "Chris."

"So what do you want to do about this?"

"Do?"

"What do you want to see happen?"

Chris waved his hand. "Ah, nothing. De minimis non curat lex."

I smiled. "The law does not concern itself with trifles."

"You know Latin?"

"I'm pretty good with it. You?"

Chris shook his head. "Just a few legal phrases. Res ipsa

loquitur."

"The thing speaks for itself," I said.

"Exactly," Chris said.

"Law student?"

"Guilty."

"Where?" I said.

"UCLA," Chris said.

"What year?"

"Third."

"Got a job lined up?"

"Public defender's office."

"Criminal defense, huh?"

He nodded. "I want to be in a courtroom."

"Man," I said, "I wouldn't want to be a baby DA going up against you."

"You a lawyer by any chance?"

"I work for one. As an investigator. In fact, we have a criminal matter right now, a juvenile case."

"You still do any fighting?" Chris asked.

"Why do you ask?"

"What you did to me," Chris said. "A full nelson, right? It was like the jaws of death."

"No offense, I hope," I said.

"Only embarrassment," Chris said.

"You want to come back here?"

"To work out? Yeah, I'd like to."

"I'll see what I can do."

I talked it over with Jimmy. He agreed to let Chris come back. Then Jimmy went to White Guy, whose name was Terrence, and told him he was banned for six months, and if he ever wanted back in he'd better come with an apology and a better attitude.

Situation handled. Without a riot. What a novel idea.

Chris wanted to talk to me about criminal law and investigation, so we had some Gatorade and chatted. Jimmy came by and I asked him if he had a lead on San Dae-Ho. Jimmy said no.

Chris said, "I know that guy. He works out at Pereira Dojo on Devonshire."

"How well do you know him?" I asked.

"Not much. I just know he's got a rep."

"It was good I ran into you, Chris," I said.

"You *rammed* into me," Chris said.

"Guilty," I said.

I drove to the Pereira Dojo. I parked on Devonshire and walked to the entrance, looked through the glass. There was a workout going on inside.

No one in there matched the description of San Dae-Ho.

I got back in Spinoza and made a U to the other side of the street, parking directly across from the dojo for a bit of unglamorous surveillance. After an hour I gave up and thought about driving back to the beach. It just seemed a shame to end an official trip to the Valley with a goose egg. Mandi McGuane was not much help. Shane McGuane and his buds were a complete bust. But it was getting into late afternoon, and there really wasn't anywhere to—

—that's when the thought hit me and jacked up my pulse. I took a deep breath and called Sophie.

"Hello?"

"It's Mike."

"Well hi."

I liked the way she said *hi*.

I said, "So... want to talk about my guest appearance?"

"Absolutely," she said.

"What would be a good time?"

"Any day after three-thirty or so. Or the weekend."

"Would today be too soon? I'm in the Valley."

"Today would work. How far away are you?"

"I don't know. I'm at Devonshire and Reseda."

"Hm, probably twenty-five minutes, half an hour." She gave me the address. "I'll leave word at the office that you're coming to see me."

The Constantine Academy occupied a prime piece of real estate in Tarzana. It was flashback time for me, as the design of the place was Ivy League. The tuition, no doubt, was of similar magnitude.

The office receptionist had my name on a list. She gave me a visitor tag and directions to Sophie's room. I walked past a grass field where soccer practice was going on. Looked like eighth graders. Their practice uniforms were sharper than my best clothes, though that bar is not particularly high.

On the other side was a nice rose garden inside a brick edging. Pink floribunda from the look of it. I approved.

I turned a corner at Room 11. Using my powers of deduction, I found Room 12. The blinds were open. I saw Sophie sitting at a desk in the front of the room, looking over papers.

I opened the door. Sophie looked up. "Mike."

I liked the way she said my name. I was liking the way she said anything.

She stood and said, "Come on in."

I came in. And looked around. The room was decorated with book-themed posters. *Don Quixote, Huckleberry Finn, Animal Farm, Moby Dick.*

"What do you think?" Sophie said.

"I think this is a good room in which to think," I said.

"We encourage that."

"It'd be nice if they encouraged that in the public schools."

"Easy now," she said.

"Socrates would have taken hemlock a lot sooner if he had to take orders from the LAUSD."

She smiled.

And yes, I loved the way she did that, too.

"How'd you get this gig?" I said.

"A friend of mine teaches fourth grade here. When something opened up in the middle school she recommended me."

"You like it?"

"Love it. Class sizes are just right."

"You have a favorite?"

"Eighth grade English."

"What are you into right now?"

"We just finished *Julius Caesar*, and now it's *The Wednesday Wars*."

"I don't think I know that one."

"Coming-of-age story. About a boy who discovers the wonders of Shakespeare."

"Imagine that," I said. "A teacher who wants kids interested in Shakespeare."

"So you approve?"

"O let my books be then the eloquence of my speaking breast."

"I'll take that as a yes."

"With a little help from sonnet twenty-three."

She smiled again, the warm and inviting kind, the kind that a red-blooded American man before the MeToo age would have taken and run with. Music rising, take her in your arms. Long, satisfying kiss.

I cleared my throat and said, "At least I think it was twenty-three."

Was there a hint of disappointment in her eyes?

"Well now," I said. "What am I to tell your young charges?"

"I thought it would be nice for them to meet someone with a classical education who is now doing interesting work."

"I assume without the part about the occasional breaking of bones."

"You think you can nuance that?"

"For you, I could nuance an elephant stampede."

She smiled and looked down.

We were silent for a long moment.

I said, "Speaking of elephants..."

Sophie looked up, puzzled.

"There's a great big one sitting in this room," I said.

She got it. "I know."

"I think it's going to follow us around until we, um, dispatch it."

"And how do you propose we do that?"

"Well, you know what they say about how you eat an elephant?"

"One bite at a time," she said.

"How about we take it that way, one bite at a time?"

"I'd like that," she said.

I pushed my heart back down from my throat to my chest.

"And speaking of bites, may I take you out for a sumptuous meal?"

"What did you have in mind?"

"I was thinking In-N-Out."

"With animal-style fries?"

"Naturally."

"How can I resist?"

W e ate in the car in the parking lot, but for me it was like being in the Eiffel Tower overlooking Paris. When I dropped her back at the Constantine Academy, I felt like a small chunk of the elephant had been dispatched. There was still a lot of pachyderm to go, so I asked if I could take her for a drive on Saturday. She said that would be nice.

I t was getting on toward sunset when I got back to Paradise Cove. I put on KJAZZ 88.1, plopped on the sofa. It was a peaceful five minutes. Then my phone buzzed.

Ira said, "Where are you?"

"Home again, home again jiggity—"

"Michael, listen."

"Okay, boss."

"Clint Cunningham hanged himself."

T here's a reason they call it a gut punch. I got plenty of those physically in the cage. When you get news like this, out of the blue, you feel it in the same region of your body.

I sat up.

Ira said, "He didn't succeed, thank God."

"He's alive?"

"I just got notified. He's in the infirmary at juvi."

"So... wait, wasn't there a hearing today?"

"It was taken off calendar when Clint didn't show.

Which means we still represent him."

"What are we supposed to do?"

"I asked that notification of Clint's parents be left to me. You've met with both. Do you have any suggestions?"

I thought about it. "It would be a good idea for someone to be with Trista when she hears it. I'll go."

"Give it to her tomorrow morning. Let her sleep. They won't let her see him anyway and there's nothing she can do now. What about the father?"

"I'll leave a message with his office."

"Why is that?"

"He's not the warmest of men," I said.

I went outside and sat on my porch. The sound of ocean waves echoed through the cove. Usually that's a comfort. Tonight it was a reminder that human life is evanescent and the sea is forever. We're here for a short time and should make a difference for the good before we dissolve into the earth. So you try with a kid like Clint Cunningham, but he tries for a fast exit. You feel powerless. You feel like you let him down. You feel like there's no point in trying anymore if that's all you get from the effort.

But then, if you keep listening, the sea will remind you of something else. It didn't erode rocks and make beaches by giving up. You've got to admire the perseverance. So you decide to be like the sea.

I called Trista Cunningham in the morning. I told her I wanted to update her on Clint's case, and asked if it might be convenient if I stopped by.

"Is something wrong?" she said.

"Clint is making a motion to represent himself."

"A motion?"

"In court. The hearing was supposed to be yesterday. It's better if I explain in person."

Pause. "All right."

The drive was torturous. I kept going over in my head the right thing to say. I've never been good at that sort of thing. Ira says it's because there's an ice ring around my heart. Maybe he's right. At least this wasn't a death notice. Only once did I deliver that kind of news, or rather went along with the deliverer. It was back when I worked for Joey Feint. He was hired by a husband and wife in New Haven to find their missing daughter, age 16. They thought she'd run away because there'd been a lot of fighting about boyfriends and school.

It wasn't like that at all.

In fact, she'd been kidnapped, raped and murdered by a neighbor of the couple, a forty-year-old accountant with a spotless resume. Joey cracked the case, found the body, called the cops, and went to deliver the news. I watched a man and woman fall apart and felt powerless to do anything about it, though I knew exactly what they were feeling. That scar tissue never goes away.

Life is all about scars. It's what you do in spite of them that counts. That doesn't make delivering news like this any easier.

Trista answered the door. "Come on in, I've just got to finish one thing. There's coffee in the kitchen. Help yourself."

She went back to her computer. "I'll just be a second."

"No rush," I said, more to myself than to her.

I went into the kitchen. A cup was waiting for me by the coffee maker. I poured some, took a sip. I put both my hands around the cup, letting it warm me. Then I headed back to the living room.

Trista was tapping away, looking hard at the monitor.

I sat. The house smelled lightly of lavender. A good thing. *Lavandula angustifolia*, English lavender, is used in aromatherapy to soothe and relax. I got the impression the smell was coming from an essential oil diffuser. Good, bring it on. She's going to need it.

"Done," she said, and closed her laptop. "Sorry."

"No need to apologize," I said.

She came over and sat in the chair opposite me. "So what's going on? It's driving me crazy not to be able to talk to Clint. Is there any way he can get out of there?"

"We'll get to that," I said. I put my cup on the coffee table. At that moment I thought about all those movies where the guy says, "Give it to me straight, Doc." I wished this was only a movie.

"Trista, last night we got some news—"

"What news?" She knew it was bad.

"They told us Clint tried to hang himself."

Trista's hand went to her mouth.

"He's all right," I said, stretching the truth. "He's in the infirmary."

"Oh God!" Trista stood. She walked around her chair and faced me again. She balled her hands into fists and pressed them against her head. "I need to see him!"

"We'll work to make that happen," I said.

"I want to see him *now*."

"I know," I said. "They have procedures. As I say—"

"That's outrageous! That's so…" Her words trailed off, replaced by heaving sobs. She turned her back to me, as if embarrassed.

For a second I was frozen. Then I went to her, wanting to put my hand on her shoulder. But I held back. She turned around. And put her head on my chest, crying.

I held her for a moment, then guided her back to the

chair and sat her down. I went into the kitchen and poured a cup of coffee. I came back and put the cup in her hands. There was a box of Kleenex on her computer table. I brought it to her.

"Thanks," she said.

"Anything I can do for you?"

"Can you stay awhile?" she said.

"Sure."

"You're my only link to Clint."

"You'll see him soon," I said.

"It's torture," she said. "Do you have kids?"

"No."

"It's hard." She dabbed her eyes with a tissue. "I sometimes think, was it worth it? And then I hate myself for thinking that."

"Don't hate yourself," I said. "I imagine every mother has that thought at one time or another. Always the question is, what do we do with our thoughts? Some people give up, some people keep going. You strike me as a keep going type."

"Thank you for saying that. You seem like a wise man."

"I think you need a long, gray beard to be one of those."

She smiled slightly. "May I ask you something?"

"Of course."

"How did you become this, an investigator?"

"Ira Rosen is a good friend of mine," I said. "I needed the work."

"But you..."

"Yes?"

"You seem... did you attend college?"

"Never graduated," I said.

"You mean you dropped out?"

I nodded.

"What college was it?" she asked.

"It doesn't matter," I said.

She looked surprised. "I'm sorry. I didn't meant to pry."

"It's a part of my life that's over and done with," I said.

"I understand," she said with a tinge of sadness.

"Yale," I said.

"Wow," she said.

"Not as big a wow as people think. It's a place like any other place, captive to the times."

"What do you mean?"

"It was originally established for the education of young men into the ministry. The first rector was the Reverend Abraham Pierson."

"Is he famous?"

"Only to people who like to read memorial plaques."

"I guess it's not training ministers anymore."

"There's a divinity school," I said.

Trista must have picked up subtext in my voice, because she leaned forward and said, "Were you part of it?"

"My mother was," I said. "She taught there."

"Your mother sounds extremely interesting."

"She was," I said.

"She's dead?"

"Yes."

"I can tell you miss her."

"Every day."

"And your father?"

"Same."

"I'm... I keep saying I'm sorry."

"That's all right," I said. "We'd have a better world if more people said it."

We sat in silence for awhile, the kind that happens when two people realize a certain bond has formed, forged out of shared suffering. There's no need for words then. Just the comfort of quiet—the welcome, momentary peace of knowing you're not alone.

I took the 101 back to Hollywood. The drive through the Cahuenga Pass brings you out where the first thing you see is the Capitol Records Building. It was built in the 50s and designed to look like a stack of records. Wonder what kids looking at it today think. A stack of Eggo waffles maybe?

Just past that is the Gower offramp. I got off, turned left and then right on Franklin and took that all the way to Los Feliz.

Ira was working at the computer when I came in.

"Be with you in a moment, lad," he said. "Pour yourself some tea." He nodded at the pot on the corner of the desk.

I got a cup from the kitchen and came back and poured. "What brew is it today?"

"Morning Thunder," Ira said. "A mix of black tea and roasted maté."

"You need your own podcast," I said. "Tea and Talmud with Ira Rosen."

"Be quiet for five minutes, please."

I went to his bookshelf and browsed. Ira had two copies of *Fahrenheit 451*, paperbacks with different cover art. I took the one that had the figure of a man dressed in paper pages that were on fire. I took it and my tea to the window bench and opened to the first page.

I t *was a pleasure to burn.*

It was a special pleasure to see things eaten, to see things blackened and changed. With the brass nozzle in his fists, with this great python spitting its venomous kerosene upon the world, the blood pounded in his head, and his hands were the hands of some amazing conductor playing all the symphonies of blazing and burning to bring down the tatters and charcoal ruins of history.

I couldn't help making a noise that sounded like *Hmmm*.
"How's that?" Ira said.

"Just murmuring," I said.

"My experience in life has taught me that a murmur is the product of a stimulus."

"Bradbury. *Fahrenheit 451*."

"Ah," said Ira. "He said he was not writing to predict the future, but to prevent it."

"Too bad it didn't work," I said.

"Drink your tea."

I read a few more pages and then Ira was finished. He wheeled over to me and asked how it went with Trista Cunningham.

I told him.

Ira shook his head. "She's a decent woman with a son in absolute despair. Remember what Gertrude Stein told Hemingway? You are a lost generation. I wonder what she'd make of Clint's generation."

"At least Stein's lost generation read books," I said. "Now everything is TikTok and World of Warcraft."

"Whatever happened to marbles and mumblety-peg?"

"I was into Jenga. Which seems appropriate."

"Why?"

"Because everything around us is on the verge of toppling, including civilization. And the people pulling out the blocks are all thumbs."

"Our task, then, is to be out there on the battlefield, helping one client and his mother, while we are still counsel of record."

"It's killing her that she can't see him."

"I've applied for an emergency order to see our client in the juvenile infirmary. I put Trista Cunningham's name in as well. Should get an answer later today."

"I talked with Gavin McGuane's parents," I said.

"In Simi?"

"The mother lives there. Mandi McGuane. Big shot real estate agent, and lives like one. She didn't offer much. I have a feeling she's withholding a lot."

"About what?" Ira said.

"Her son. He has all the earmarks of the spoiled rich kid. Mandi McGuane got a little testy with me when I mentioned it."

"Testy? With you? What a shock."

"Shane McGuane got testy, too."

"Where did you talk to him?"

"Tab's Hot Dogs," I said.

"A hot dog place?"

"A hot dog *palace*. Very good selection. He was there with three buddies of his, stuntmen types."

Ira rubbed the bridge of his nose. "I'm almost afraid to ask."

"Shane was not helpful. His stuntmen friends were not sympathetic to my entreaties."

"Michael, did you...?"

I knew what he meant. We've had this conversation many times before. "They made the first move."

Ira closed his eyes.

"It didn't go down to the wire," I said. "When one of them pulled a knife, I—"

"Knife!"

"—picked up a chair and—"

"Chair?"

"—then McGuane called them off. He didn't want the publicity."

"A blessing in disguise," Ira said.

"So those interviews were not, shall we say, fruitful. I also spent some time staking out the dojo where that guy named San Dae-Ho goes, but he didn't show up."

"Tread carefully, Michael. There is still a chance we will be removed from this case, and that incident will be moot."

"I don't call it moot when somebody comes to my house."

"By which you mean, you're turning this into a personal matter."

"I didn't do the turning," I said.

"You'll recall what the rabbi Jesus said about turning the other cheek."

"Jesus didn't live in Los Angeles."

"Useless!"

That startled me. Ira doesn't get that tone of voice very often. I know I keep pushing him to that edge.

"Don't give up on me, Ira," I said.

He took a few breaths, then said, "Back to our client. I cracked through the password on his laptop. Nothing of note. Seems this is a school computer, and he uses it mainly for that purpose. A few games, a few searches a teenage boy might be into."

"Such as?"

"Victoria's Secret," Ira said. "It's what *Playboy* magazine was back in the 1950s. We've made such strides." He shook his head. "Now about the skull drawing."

"Yes?"

The notebook was on the corner of Ira's desk. He got it and opened to the picture.

"It's that letter D," Ira said. "The snake coiling around it. Coming out of the mouth. Fangs. I think the D stands for Death, or Dead."

I thought about it. "Then the letters in the eye sockets could be somebody's name."

"Or names."

I looked at the drawing. T and B. "Two different people?"

"Michael, what are Clint's parents' names?"

It hit me. "Trista and Brian."

The awful implication sat there between us, coiled like the snake in the picture.

"We need to talk to Clint," I said.

"Best if Trista's not with us. This would not be a good thing for her to find out right now."

Ira's landline rang. He went to his desk and picked up.

"Ira Rosen....oh, yes Ms. Wynn..." Ira looked at me. "Yes, as a matter of fact, he's right here. I'll put him on."

He held out the phone. "Deputy D.A. on that knife matter."

I took it. "Romeo here."

"Hello, Mr. Romeo. My name is Hope Wynn, and I'll be handling the Sammie Sand preliminary hearing. Is this a good time to talk?"

"Sure."

"My witnesses will be you and Detective Coltrane Smith."

"Okay."

"According to Detective Smith's summary report, you are the only one who actually saw Mr. Sand draw the knife."

"I saw it in his hand, yes."

"And then you followed him into the bookstore and threw a book at him, hitting him in the head."

"A nice, big hardback."

"Mr. Romeo, I hope we can get through your testimony without difficulty."

Ira was frowning at me, as if he knew exactly what the D.D.A. was saying.

"Just lead me through it, counselor," I said.

"Now about the part where you slammed Mr. Sand's head on the floor."

"The first time?"

Pause, as if she was reviewing the report. "Yes, it seems it was three times. Would you mind explaining that to me?"

"The perp was not cooperative. He was cursing like a stevedore—"

"A what?"

"Guy who loads and unloads ships at the dock."

"Go on."

"And there were kids in the store, so I grabbed his hair and gave his head a little floor wax."

"A little?"

"The first time. The second time, because he wasn't shutting up, I was less gentle."

"And the third?"

"For emphasis."

Ira rubbed his eyes.

"This is going to be a problem," said Hope Wynn.

"For who?"

"Both of us. It's not going to sound good to the judge and it could taint the rest of your testimony."

"So what do you propose?"

"I propose that you think back and see if there was any other reason you might have had for injuring the man you had subdued."

"Injuring?" I said. "I think I knocked some sense into him."

Ira glared.

"Mr. Romeo, please—"

"I was mad, I'll admit it. I don't like men with knives attacking people or spewing garbage in front of little kids."

"But you're okay with kids watching you slam his head on the floor?"

"Excuse me, is this a cross-examination?"

"You bet it is. This is what the defense counsel is going to be asking you. I want to see how we can bring it up first, before the defense. Dull the impact for the judge."

"Those were my reasons," I said. "I don't have any more to add."

Pause.

Hope Wynn said, "We are not adversaries, Mr. Romeo."

"Good," I said.

Ira glowered.

To escape Ira's ire, which is the engine behind his glower, and to cool down from feeling like a dancing monkey on the D.A.'s string, I took a walk around the old neighborhood. I headed for the row of businesses where the Argo Bookstore had once been. It was there I first met Sophie, in another time and place. The coffee house that was on the corner was boarded up and a big FOR LEASE sign stapled to the wood.

Yes, I'm sure there are just a ton of small businesses hankering to open up a new brick-and-mortar floor space right now, what with the—

—timing is everything. Turning the corner I ran smack into a street crowd.

In LA, you can't tell your protests without a program. There's the peaceful protest, the mostly peaceful protest, the riot, and the rampage.

Your peaceful protest obeys the law and makes speeches

at places like City Hall and MacArthur Park.

Your mostly peaceful protest is a euphemism. It's what the news media calls a mob that breaks out into a riot or rampage, but they don't want the folks at home to get worked up over it.

Your riot is a physical fight between sides. One side might have started as a peaceful protest, while another side decides to break up that peace by busting some heads, causing the formerly peaceful side to respond in kind or run away like antelope from a pack of ravenous hyenas.

Your rampage is a mob that burns buildings and cars, and bloodies innocent bystanders, in an effort to create a more just society.

I didn't have a program with me, so I asked a young woman wearing a pink headband, "What's this about?"

"The city's trying to break up a camp!" she said. "Those are people! They're self-sufficient!"

I raised an eyebrow.

"Join us!" she said, waving at me to follow.

"No thanks," I said, adding, "Keep it peaceful. God bless the First Amendment."

She looked at me with a mixture of scorn and confusion. Maybe the words *God* and *First Amendment* threw her. And then, in an exhibition of today's civil discourse, she raised her middle finger at me and walked on, shouting some slogan or other.

I kept walking and saw on a side street what's called "the police presence." There were several black-and-whites, and officers in riot gear. They were about thirty yards from the passing crowd, and doing what they've been told to do, which is stand down.

The protestors shouted various epithets at them and made more finger gestures.

Just before I went on my eye caught the movement of a

thin reed. It was a guy, actually, very skinny and wearing a Jesse James bandana over his grill. He had a bottle of water in his hand. This he threw at the police officers with as much heat as he could muster. Which wasn't much in the physical sense of things. His arms were thin and smooth, his delivery delicate. If he even knew how to grip a football he probably couldn't have heaved it more than fifteen yards.

The bottle thudded on the street in front of the cops. That's when I knew it was rock solid, the water probably mostly frozen.

No harm done.

But then he reached into his backpack and pulled another bottle out, and made ready to throw again. When his arm went back I grabbed it. My fingers went all the way around his wrist.

"Hey!" Water Bottle Boy shouted.

I removed the bottle from his hand.

"Don't do that," I said.

He started spewing a load of trash, comparing me to a bodily orifice, telling me what I should do to myself, and so on.

I popped him one on the nose.

Down he went like a snipped calla lily.

A woman's voice shouted, "Did you see that? Get him!"

A dozen pairs of eyes turned toward me.

From out of this rabble came another of the thin-reed set, a brave warrior with a mask, swinging a chain with a heavy lock on the end of it. He twirled it above his head like some hopped-up Argentine gaucho, and came at me.

The flail is a weapon that almost certainly was not widely used when it was supposed to—in medieval times. Fantasy gamers love it because it looks so good in a monster's hand. But your soldier of yore figured out pretty quick that a heavy ball on the end of a chain was as likely to conk him or a fellow soldier on the bean as it was any part of the enemy. The more stable mace could be used as a club. Not so the flail. Thus we say that an out-of-control fighter was just "flailing away" at his opponent.

The gut instinct when a chain and lock come at you is to back away. Always the wrong move. It gives control to the assailant who can reach out with the chain. You have to come inside.

Or fake it.

Which is what the rocker step is for. You lunge as if to move forward, but then you plant your lead foot and push back on it. Like you're on a rocking chair. You want to cause momentary confusion, especially if the other guy has a weapon.

So Chain Boy came at me with enthusiasm, swinging the thing over his head.

I watched the rotations, timing them.

And then made my move, issuing hearty abdominal *kiai* —Karate scream—as I lunged.

My attacker's whole body flinched. The lock missed me but caught the guy's knee, flush. He screamed like a five-year-old, grabbing his knee and dropping the chain.

Which I picked up.

Just in time, too, as four or five other peaceful marchers came at me with various implements. A skinny guy—why were they all so skinny?—held a water bottle like a club. Frozen or not, it can do a lot of damage if it catches you across the face. A woman who looked like she weighed about as much as her backpack held her backpack by the straps, ready to lash out with it. And a third runt, amazingly, had nunchucks. Nunchucks! The very symbol of peace in our time!

And there was me, keeping them at bay with a chain and lock, whirling it around my head.

For a moment, over a no-man's-land of five feet, we faced each other.

And then it seemed like the whole parade gathered around, like spectators in the Roman Colosseum. They were rooting for the lions. Talking trash.

I was trying to decide which wimp to take out first, when the decision was taken away from me.

A phalanx of riot police moved in, shields up, getting between me and these upstanding citizens.

And then in a display of breathtaking urban alchemy, the crowd turned its attention away from me and started shouting at the police. A fog of F-words befouled the air.

A water bottle bounced off a cop's polycarbonate shield.

The riot squad pushed forward.

A girl screamed, "Police brutality! Police brutality!"

And there I was, behind a wall of police, holding a flail.

"You!" It was one of the cops, pointing at me with his billy.

"Weapon down, now!" he shouted.

I dropped the chain and spread out my arms.

The cop motioned for me to come forward.

I complied.

"Arms behind you," the cop said.

"Excuse me?" I said.

"I'm going to cuff you."

"Excuse me again."

"Let's make this look good." The cop took the cuffs off his Sam Browne. "This is for your protection."

I turned around and allowed myself to be cuffed. Then

he took me by the arm and started leading me away from the mayhem.

"You'll never get away with this, copper!" I said.

"Don't overplay it," the cop said.

That's how I ended up in the back of a police van. All cage work and Plexiglas. Hard seats, made for easy cleaning because you never know what's going to come out of the body of an arrestee. At least these seats had a concave space in the lower back area so a guy with cuffs on has a place for his hands.

All the comforts afforded an arrestee. Though at 6'4" and 230, I was a bit cramped.

Out the window I watched the ongoing street theatre. It's all rehearsed. The mob lives for scenes like this. Getting the police into confrontation mode is good drama, with lots of juicy clips for the evening news. I couldn't help thinking of Gandhi then, and Martin Luther King, contrasting their nonviolent resistance with the foul-mouthed, bottle-throwing mayhem happening now.

But where Gandhi and King had reasonable arguments, based on the objective truth of human worth, this new form of protest went for blood first, power second, and nothing else third. Where we end up is anybody's guess.

After half an hour the cop who cuffed me came back to the van. He had his helmet and riot gear off. He was around thirty or so, not tall but in good shape. He slipped into the seat next to me. He was holding the chain and lock.

"You okay?" he said.

"Swell," I said.

"I'm Officer Aoki. I want you to tell me about this." He held up the chain.

"That's a homemade flail," I said.

"I know. Popular item with some of the demonstrators. I want to know why you had this."

"I took it off a guy," I said. "He came at me with it."

"Can you explain why?"

"Because he is an amoral thug."

Aoki couldn't help smiling. "Other than that."

"You mean a stimulus for his thuggery? Well, it could have been that I gave a Chicago free lunch to one of his companions."

"A what?"

"A punch in the nose. He was going to throw a water bottle at you guys."

"And you stopped him?"

"It seemed like a good idea at the time. Then the crowd started to turn on me, and the guy with that flail was front and center."

Tapping his leg with his fingers, Aoki said, "That's your story?"

"Facts," I said. "You want to canvass for witnesses?"

"Um, no. Let's file this one under no harm, no foul."

I nodded. "How about taking off the bracelets?"

"I better drive you away first," Aoki said. "Remove you from the scene. Where can I drop you?"

"At my employer's house," I said.

"Which is where?"

I told him.

He said, "We're going to take the long way."

As he drove east on Prospect, I asked what this dustup was all about.

"The Shakespeare Bridge Garden," he said.

I'd been across the bridge a few times. It's a gothic-style concrete bridge built in 1926 and named for the Bard.

About twenty years ago the city council and local home-owners sought to resist a growing homeless encampment under the bridge by making it a garden spot. Flowers and shrubs and ivy moved in, while the overnight guests were moved out with a little help from the cops.

"But in the last year, you know," Aoki said, "there's homeless camps all over the city. And a new one under the bridge. That's what this was all about."

"The graffiti is back, too," I said.

Aoki shook his head. "Yep. All over. All over those great murals downtown on the 101. Can't be stopped."

"Won't be, you mean."

My driver said nothing. We took a circuitous route up to Los Feliz Boulevard, then headed back toward Ira's. Other than the flying bottles and chains, it was a lovely day in L.A.

We pulled up in front of Ira's. Officer Aoki got out street side, opened the door, had me lean forward. He unlocked the cuffs and I stepped out to join him.

He closed the door and faced me. "Interesting day."

"Indeed," I said. "In case you need to follow up..." I fished for my wallet to get one of Ira's cards. My hands were a little numb from the cuffs, and I dropped it.

I bent to pick it up.

And heard a distant *crack*.

I stood.

Aoki went down, blood spattering.

A nother crack, and a bullet pinged the police car an inch from my arm.

I grabbed Aoki's shirt collar and dragged him around the SUV.

"Michael?"

It was Ira, with his braces, standing at the front door.

I waved my arm. "Shooter! Officer down! Call it in!"

He didn't need to be told twice.

I looked at Aoki, who was face up but with lights out. I ripped his shirt open. There was an ugly red hole in the heart area. I whipped off my shirt and balled it up and pressed it to the wound.

"What goes on here?" It was Ira's neighbor, the widow Mrs. Morgenstern, standing right outside her front door.

"Go back inside, Mrs. Morgenstern! Back inside now!"

"Don't you tell me what to do." She shook her finger at me.

"Somebody's shooting!"

"Who?" she said. "Why is there a police car—"

"Get inside now or I'll rip your dress off!"

Who knows where inspiration comes from? Why that perverse phrase came out of me I don't know, but I'm sure it had something to do with my previous knowledge of Mrs. Morgenstern's personality, and what would likely cause her the most shock.

Whatever, it worked. She huffed once and retreated indoors. I was reasonably sure she'd call the police, too.

"Hang on." I didn't know if Aoki could hear me, but it was worth a try. I was knocked out once, early in my cage career, and three days later woke up in a hospital. During the blackout I thought I heard my manager say, "Don't leave me, Mike. We've got too much money to make." When I asked him about that later, his mouth flopped open. "Those were my exact words," he said.

To Aoki I said, "Help is coming. Stay with me."

From just inside the screen door, Ira said, "Where's the shooter?"

"I don't know," I said. "Across the street, maybe."

"How's the officer?"

"Hole in the chest."

"I'm coming."

"No—"

But there was to be no argument. A police officer was critically wounded and that's all Ira needed to know.

Keeping one hand pressing on his chest I unholstered Aoki's sidearm, a Glock. The extractor was above surface, indicating a round in the chamber.

Ira's screen door swung open, and out he came, moving fast on his braces and holding a first aid kit.

No shots fired.

Ira got to me and lowered himself to his knees. He opened the kit and ripped open a packet, took out a small cloth.

"Take away your shirt," he said.

He used the cloth to clean around the wound. Blood wasn't gushing, a good sign.

Then he took out a larger packet and opened it. He peeled off a backing and placed what looked like a piece of plastic over the hole.

"Chest seal," Ira said. "Keeps air from being sucked in."

He put his ear to Aoki's mouth. Then he touched the neck. "No jugular vein distension."

"What about the shooter?" I said.

"Stay right where you are," Ira said.

"He wasn't after the cop."

"I know."

Five minutes later the first black-and-white arrived, lights and sirens. It took up a position on the street, ready for threat assessment.

They called Ira.

"South side of the street," Ira said.

An officer got out of the passenger side and knelt beside the unit, gun at the ready. His partner joined him.

Officer Aoki breathed steadily. And opened his eyes.

"Don't move," Ira said. "You've been shot."

"Chest," Aoki said.

"Missed the heart," Ira said.

Aoki moved his eyes to mine.

"Thank you," he said.

Soon the neighborhood was locked down. Mrs. Morgenstern was reduced to shouting various forms of *Get off my lawn* from her front window.

A couple of medics took over the care of Aoki. A two-person field unit from LAPD's Scientific Investigation Division arrived.

Officers canvassed the homes.

One of the SID investigators was named Monica Helberg, fiftyish and fit. She had me walk through the shooting from the moment I got out of the vehicle.

She examined the bullet hole in the passenger-side door.

She turned and traced a line in the air with her finger.

"Downward," she said. "Most likely it came from that parking structure."

The top of which we could see, but it was one heck of a long way away.

"Sniper level," I said.

"And you think you were the target?"

"Certainly not Officer Aoki. This took planning."

"And what would be the motive?"

"Some people want me dead," I said.

"And you know this how?"

"Experience," I said. "It's happened before."

She cleared her throat. "Is there a place we can talk?"

We went into Ira's and sat at the kitchen table. Ira made tea and told her she didn't have to wear a mask in here. She took it off with a relieved smile, and explained her role in performing scientific field investigation and the taking of statements from relevant witnesses. She'd been a detective with Central Division.

Which is why she led with, "First off, who exactly are you thinking of when you say some people want you dead?"

"Unfortunately," I said, "people I can't ID. Well, maybe one. I'm chief witness against a guy named Sammie Sand. It's a knife attack case. I've been told he's from a family of wastrels."

"Of what?"

"He talks that way sometimes," Ira said.

"Thugs," I said. "Criminals. No-goodniks."

"I get it," Helberg said.

"The prelim's coming up," I said.

Helberg nodded. "Other than that case, who else can you think of?"

"Mr. Rosen and I have a juvenile client. It's a drug beef. We were warned to drop him."

"By who?"

"We don't know," I said. "Whoever it was hired somebody to deliver the message. This messenger brought along an enforcer."

"A very big enforcer," Ira said, "whom Michael dispatched."

"What do you mean, dispatched?" Helberg said.

"I had to knock him out," I said.

"With your fist?"

"No, with Poseidon. I have a statuette of Poseidon in my petunia garden."

Helberg blinked a couple of times. "Continue."

"Whoever it was who hired the muscle, we don't know.

Even he doesn't know."

"You questioned him?"

"I brought him to his crib and put him to bed."

Shaking her head, Helberg said, "I'm having trouble following this."

"Welcome to the club," Ira said.

"What I mean," I said, "is that when he came around we had a chance to talk."

"He just talked to you?"

"Well, I had him handcuffed to a pipe, but he was reasonable. And hurt. I had a doctor look at him."

In a motion that implied extreme interest, Helberg raised her eyebrows as high as they could go.

"She lives in my mobile home park at Paradise Cove. She gave him some first aid and told me I was responsible for him."

"O...K," Helberg said.

"He took this on as a freelance job, and doesn't know who did the ultimate hire. So it was planned out, like the snipe that just took place."

"So no theories on who it might be?"

"I've interviewed some people on this case who were not exactly friendly."

"Any names?"

"I'll give you a list," Ira said.

"Fine," Helberg said. "But you probably surmise that without more we won't be able to get a warrant on anyone. And resources and time factor into any questioning."

"What about the bullet?"

"We'll analyze it, of course, but won't get much from that unless we can match it to a profile in the data banks."

"If only this were TV," I said. "You'd have a pristine lab and solve the whole thing in fifty minutes."

Helberg sighed.

. . .

After the interview I sat at Ira's window and watched the activity outside dying down.

Dying.

Down.

The whole city was circling the drain. And everybody knew it, even the people pulling the levers of power. They just put on blinders and spoke sweet nothings into microphones.

"You seem gloomier than usual, Michael."

I turned to Rabbi Rosen. "Me? Gloomy?"

"Tell Uncle Ira what's burdening you."

"Other than the state of mankind, madness unleashed, and nihilism in the air?"

"Pish. Read Genesis again and you'll have no surprises on any of that. But you will have the beginning of an answer."

"Burn me a bush," I said.

"That's Exodus," Ira said.

"You're our new *Jeopardy* champion," I said.

"The air has grown cold."

"Let me guess," I said. "Because I have an ice ring around my heart?"

"We've had this conversation before, haven't we?"

"It's no better now than the first time," I said.

"I think you like having it," Ira said.

I didn't respond.

"Keeps you from getting close to people," Ira said. "Or people getting close to you."

"You're four feet away from me."

"You're not going to clever your way out of this one," Ira said.

"Time for me to go," I said, and stood.

"Don't act as if you don't care."

"Do I?"

"Very much. You care about Sophie. You care about Clint Cunningham."

I went to the door.

"We have an appointment to see Clint tomorrow," Ira said.

"Good luck with that," I said and shut the door behind me.

I took three steps.

And stopped.

I went back, opened the door, stuck my head in and said, "What time?"

I drove away wondering if I was being followed. When an assassin misses you, it's only a matter of time before the next attempt.

Unless you do unto him before he does unto you.

I was tired of everything. Which made me a little loopy driving down the mean streets. Like I was hyperventilating. You don't see straight. You don't clearly see the guy in the crosswalk you almost hit. You do hear him cuss you out, and that brings you back to your senses.

It was heading to later afternoon. Schools—the ones that were meeting on-site, that is—would be getting out. Most public schools were locked down tight. The teachers' union wasn't interested in having their members do any on-site work. Better to Zoom from home in their pajamas and collect the paychecks.

But Elias Hall would be having classes.

So that's where I went. It was located in the foothills above Sherman Oaks. A school for movie stars' kids and other high-end offspring. It had an old California, hacienda-style design, with manicured lawns and gardens. Climbing ivy covered the encircling wall. The driveway entrance was guarded by a security kiosk.

I cruised a little further. On the opposite side of the street was a parking lot, enclosed by a wrought iron fence. Since there were no retail outlets around it had to be for the school. And what a collection of fine automobiles the kids got to drive.

I spotted Gavin McGuane's car there. I went up another block, turned around and parked. I turned the radio on to the news. It was cheery stuff. An ex-con from Sylmar who was being charged with killing five and wounding three others during a shooting spree in Chatsworth was pleading not guilty by reason of insanity. One of his victims was a woman who was shot while waiting to pick up a friend to go to church. He left paralyzed a Chatsworth teenager who had just dropped his girlfriend off at home.

Then there was the unnamed woman who was killed after being struck by a Metrolink train in Burbank. An investigation was ongoing. And another one of those high-speed chases L.A. is famous for, finally ending after a record-breaking six hours. Seven patrol vehicles had been in on that pursuit. When they finally nabbed him he turned out to be one of our fine, upstanding citizens with two felony warrants out on him.

At least the weather report was nice. It was 73 degrees downtown, which would make it about 78 or 80 out here in the Valley.

When it was announced that sports would be next, I clicked it off. Who cared about pro sports anymore?

Soon enough Gavin McGuane and Bianca Aiken came out of the gates of Elias with some other students. He had his arm draped over her like she was a giant stuffed pet won at a carnival. They crossed over into the parking lot. When the happy couple pulled out and headed toward Ventura Boulevard, I followed.

Gavin had the top down on his Porsche, as I did with Spinoza. We could have been in a video about the Southern California lifestyle. Just leave out the politicians, taxes, and crime stats, and you've got yourself a reason to move here.

Ten minutes later Gavin pulled into a Chick-fil-A and got in the drive-thru line. I parked at the curb and waited. As usual, there was a long string of cars. But it advanced with crisp efficiency. One thing this fowl enterprise knew was how to move customers. It wasn't too long before Gavin emerged and drove two minutes to Johnny Carson Park. That's a neat little green space across from Burbank Studios, where "The King of Late Night" did his show for so many years.

Gavin parked at the curb. I hung back as he and Bianca got out and made their way to some picnic tables. Then I parked and watched.

There were parents with kids in the play area, which was a good thing. For too long the city had cordoned off playgrounds. The experts figured keeping kids cooped up indoors was better for them than climbing around in fresh air. Gosh, how did we ever get along without experts?

I went back to watching the exciting scene of Gavin and Bianca eating their sammies. But then they were joined by a kid with long, stringy hair. He didn't sit. It looked like they all knew each other. The kid had a backpack slung over one shoulder. More talking, then the kid dug into his pocket and pulled something out. When he handed it to Bianca I saw it was a few bills, folded. Bianca handed the kid something. He put it in his pocket and hurried away.

I kept my eye on the kid. He was heading toward me, toward the cars parked along the street. I waited to see which one he went to. A white Corvette. He got in. I started up Spinoza and did a quick U and put my car next to the Vette so he couldn't pull out. I got out and walked around to his door.

He lowered the window and said, "Hey, man."

"Going to have to ask you to give it up, son," I said.

His doe eyes widened. "Huh?"

"You were under observation. I saw the transaction."

"Wait...what..."

I have found that clichés often work wonders. "We can do this the easy way, or the hard way."

His Adam's apple bobbed. "Are you security?"

"As far as you're concerned, I'm insecurity. Let's have it."

"Please don't tell my mom, please!"

"No intention of telling your mother anything, son. But I will take the contraband. Or there will be consequences."

I put out my hand.

He looked at it for a second, then back up at me. "Oh, man. If I give it to you, will you just let me go?"

"I'll certainly consider it."

Tears pooled in his eyes. He reached into his pocket and handed me... a thumb drive.

"What's this?" I said.

"Come on."

"What's on it?"

"What do you think?" he said. "Math tests. Papers."

"You're cheating?"

"Come on, it's hard."

"What is?"

"Elias."

"You're buying test answers and papers from Bianca Aiken?"

He muttered the F-word.

"How much you pay for this?" I said.

"A hundred," he said.

I whistled. "I could have played a lot of Super Mario Bros. with that, back in the day."

He blinked a couple of times.

"Now give me the drugs," I said.

"The what? No way! No drugs!"

"Going to have to search your backpack."

Defiant now, he said, "Go ahead!" He grabbed it from the passenger seat and held it out for me.

"Never mind," I said. "Here you go."

I gave him the thumb drive.

"You're letting me keep it?"

"You paid for it. But let me tell you, in the long run, it's better if you do your own work."

He frowned. "Not if I'm gonna get into Harvard."

"Tell your mom to save her money. Go to a trade school. Become a plumber or an electrician. Then you won't cheat because you can't. A clogged toilet has a way of keeping you honest."

"Can I go now?"

I made a sign of the cross at him. I got back in Spinoza, did another U, and parked in my original spot.

Then I went over to chat with Gavin and Bianca.

"Hi, kids."

Four eyes flashed at me. Half-eaten chicken sandwiches lay on wrappers on the table.

Gavin said, "Hey, what—"

"Nice day," I said.

"What are you doing here?" Bianca said.

"You know this guy?" Gavin said.

"He's some kind of lawyer."

"I will not be insulted," I said. "I only work for a lawyer."

"What do you want?" Gavin said.

"I like to see young couples in love," I said. "Gives me hope for the future."

Bianca shifted nervously, gripped Gavin's arm.

"Just wanted to ask a couple of questions," I said.

"We're eating," Gavin said.

"And a nice repast it seems," I said.

"Huh?" Gavin said.

"He talks funny," Bianca said.

"I'll keep it simple," I said. "Your classmate, Clint Cunningham, is in trouble for dealing. I just wanted to know what you might be able to tell me about that operation at Elias."

"Operation?" Gavin said.

"Drugs," I said.

"I don't know anything about that," he said.

"Surely you've heard things. A school as small as Elias doesn't have many secrets."

Gavin tried to eat a waffle fry with practiced coolness. It was too obvious.

"What about it?" I said. "If I was a student at Elias and wanted to get in on some Vector Dust, who would I talk to?"

He stopped munching. Swallowed hard.

"Look, man, I'm not into any of that," Gavin said. "I wouldn't mess up my future. I'm going to Harvard."

"Is everybody in your school hung up on going to Harvard?"

"I'm gonna be a lawyer," Gavin said.

"Be a plumber."

He seemed unable to process that thought.

"What do you *want* from us?" Bianca said. "My dad isn't going to like this."

"You don't think Clint is dealing on his own, do you?"

Gavin stuffed another fry in his mouth. "I told you we don't know anything about drugs. Clint is a freak."

"Is that what you say, Bianca?"

She looked at the table, a sad expression on her face.

Gavin said, "Look, sorry for Clint, but he shouldn't have been dealing."

"Give me a name," I said, "and I'll leave you to your repas—your lunch."

"We don't know any names," Gavin said.

"Yes, you do," I said. "Tell you what. You give me a name, and I won't report an underground traffic in homework."

That got their faces twitching.

"Yeah, I had a little chat with your latest client, right over there."

"Come on," Gavin said. "That's nothing."

"Cheating is nothing?"

"Everybody does it."

"Great training for a lawyer," I said. "Have you heard of the Canons of Ethics?"

"The what?"

"Never mind. Would the administration at Elias take the same view?"

At this point Gavin spouted a four-syllable word that was not flattering to mothers.

"Wait," Bianca said.

I waited.

"Can I talk to him?" Bianca asked.

"Sure," I said. "I'll watch your lunch and make sure the squirrels don't get it."

Bianca got up and Gavin followed. They went a few yards away and jawed. It looked like Bianca was trying to convince her boyfriend to say something. He shook his head. Bianca said some more. Gavin frowned. More talk.

They came back to the table.

"Look," Gavin said, "this is serious. If it ever got out we told you, it would be bad, really bad."

"He's not joking," Bianca said.

"Listen kids, I am a professional working for a client. I know how to keep confidences. I've never given up anyone in my life. No one will ever know you talked to me."

Gavin looked at Bianca. She nodded.

"Okay," Gavin said. "There's a guy, graduated from Elias a couple years ago. He is one bad guy. I don't know how much business he does. Please don't let him know it was me—"

"He won't know."

Gavin took a breath. "Danny Durant."

"Where can I find this Danny Durant?"

"I don't know," Gavin said. "But I did hear if you want to score, he's got guys on Hollywood Boulevard, near the Scientology building."

"They'll see you coming a mile away," Bianca said.

"Then they won't see me," I said.

"Can we eat now?" Gavin said.

Feeling a bit peckish myself, I picked up a carnitas burrito from Poquito Mas. Easy to eat on the trip back to Paradise Cove. I parked in my driveway and immediately walked over to C Dog's place. I heard rock music thumping inside. And through the screen door I saw Carter "C Dog" Weeks doing push-ups.

"How many is that?" I said.

He stopped, looked up. "Mike!"

"Mind if I come in?"

"Come on!"

He was wearing red swim trunks and nothing else. He

jumped up and extended his arm. "Feel that. Right there." He tapped the lateral head of his tricep.

I gave it a poke with my finger. "Nice," I said.

"Push-ups!" C Dog said. "You were right."

"That should not surprise you," I said.

"Man, I'm gonna be a Greek god." He put his hands on his hips, Superman style.

"Then we shall have to pick a name for you," I said.

"Let's go for it," C Dog said.

"How about Doggerel, god of rock lyrics?"

He thought about it, nodded. "I like it."

"All Greek gods need a task," I said.

"They do?"

"Sure. Like Hermes. He guided dead souls to the River Styx."

"What is that?"

"The river of the underworld," I said. "There the souls would wait for the boatman, Charon, who could ferry them across the river to Hades, but only if they had the fare."

C Dog now seemed supremely interested. He lowered himself to the floor, sitting cross-legged. "You mean you had to pay to get into Hades?"

"That's right. If you didn't have the fare, you had to wander the underworld until you could find the pauper's entrance. That's why when a man died his kin would put a coin under his tongue."

"Crazy."

I sat on his futon, so I was looking down at him like a king on a throne. "And now, O Doggerel, I have a task for you."

The god of rock raised his eyebrows.

"I want you to buy some drugs," I said.

"Whoa!"

"There's a seller who works Hollywood Boulevard

around the Scientology building. I want you to go down there and wander around—"

"I get it. Wait for a mad hatter."

"Exactly," I said.

"What's he selling?"

"Vector Dust."

"Whoa!"

"A packet'll go for about—"

"Fifty," C Dog said.

"I'll give you the money."

"Then what?"

"I'll be across the street. I just want to ID him. We'll meet up later."

"What if there's a cop around?"

"I will get you out of any trouble, my son."

"What'll I do with the drugs?"

"You will give them to me."

"Whoa! Isn't that like illegal evidence?"

"This isn't about evidence. I want to get to a guy named Danny Durant. A hatter usually makes periodic deposits during the night. I'll follow him."

"Whoa!"

"You've stopped several horses tonight."

"That's dangerous."

"But your part's easy. You just play the old C Dog. Think you can do that?"

He paused, then puffed out his chest. "I am Doggerel! I can do anything!"

"Good," I said. "I'm going to check into a motel in the Valley. I'll contact you from there."

"How come?"

"A couple of unfriendly guys found me here. I don't want to be found right now."

"Why don't you stay with me? We could—"

"Thanks anyway, Doggerel. We'll be in touch."

M oving in darkness, I got some clothes from my unit. I drove back to the Valley and checked into a Motel 6 in Canoga Park. It had a lovely view of a Valvoline Instant Oil Change next door. Tourists must come from all over the world to admire its architecture and delightful color scheme. But I kept the curtains closed and read *The Long Goodbye* until I fell asleep.

"H e doesn't want to see you," the desk deputy said. It was morning and Ira and I were back at central juvi. Ira said, "He's a minor and I'm his lawyer, acting *in loco parentis*. He is to be treated like a boy who has taken a cookie before dinner and doesn't wish to see his father. Here's a copy of the order."

Ira handed him the emergency order from the court.

"Even so, we have a responsibility here," the deputy said. His nameplate read *M. Gonzalez*. We all wore masks like obedient citizens.

"As do we, and who has the greater? The jailer or the parent? I don't want to make a stink, but I will if this order is not honored."

"He's under restraint."

"We won't be long."

The deputy told us to wait.

"He's going to talk to his supervisor," Ira said.

"Like a car salesman talks to his manager?" I said.

"Almost exactly like that. We are living in a time when justice takes a back seat to covering one's backside. It can almost tempt one to cynicism."

"Come on in," I said. "The water's fine."

"Cynicism's waters are too polluted," Ira said. "I suggest you get out while you can."

"And give up all this angst?"

"It might make you human," Ira said.

"We can't have that."

"Shmendrik."

"I love it when you talk Yiddish to me."

"Be happy I talk to you at all," Ira said.

The deputy returned to talk to us both. "Here's the way it is," M. Gonzalez said. "Ten minutes. But if he gets out of control, the interview is over."

"Agreed," said Ira.

"Follow me."

The infirmary in central juvi is not an inspiring place. Dull yellow walls, the faint smell of urine under the more powerful scent of disinfectant. A couple of beds with scratchy blankets. Clint Cunningham was on one of the beds. His right wrist was shackled to the rail. He was the only one in the room.

"He refuses to wear a mask," Deputy Gonzalez said. "Stay ten feet away."

"Why not six?" I asked.

The deputy shrugged, then went out to the hall.

Clint looked at us. "I don't want to see you."

"We won't be long, Clint," Ira said.

"I said no!"

"How are you feeling?"

He didn't answer.

"Your mother wants to know," Ira said.

Clint shook his head, then looked at the wall.

"She's understandably upset," Ira said. "Can you talk to her, through me?"

"Go away," Clint said.

"They won't let her in to see you," Ira said. "Let me take something back to her."

Clint didn't move.

"Clint?" Ira said.

No answer.

"This is useless," I said.

Ira snapped a look at me.

"Kid has no guts," I said.

"Michael!"

"Treating his mother that way," I said.

"Shut up!" Clint said.

"What's TBD?" I said.

"Michael—"

"We found the skull drawing in your notebook," I said. "I want to know what TBD means."

For a second nobody moved. Then Clint went nuts. He screamed, pulled on the bed rail, kicked, kept screaming, his body writhing as if possessed.

Deputy Gonzalez shot into the room. "What goes on?"

"As you see," Ira said.

"Interview over," Gonzalez said.

Clint kept up his antics. It was a pure tantrum, or an audition for an exorcist movie.

"Observe closely," Ira said to Gonzalez. "We asked a couple of questions, and this is what happened."

"You have to go now," Gonzalez said.

Outside, Ira said, "Your bedside manner needs improvement."

"So send me to charm school," I said.

"That would be a disaster... for the school. But you may have blundered into giving us more time."

"Do tell."

"The deputy is a witness to Clint's mental state. His screaming fit is evidence of incompetency should he attempt to replace us. He'll likely recover, so our time is not unlimited."

"Someone needs to tell his mother about the visit."

"I'll do it," Ira said.

"Good," I said. "I've got a few cages to rattle."

"What's that mean?" Ira said.

"You know, my bedside manner."

"What are you cooking up this time?" Ira said.

"I got a lead on a dealer who may be working Elias. Thought I'd try to have a little talk with him."

"You know where he is?"

"I know how to find out."

Ira sighed. "My usual admonition applies."

"Which is?"

"Don't get killed and try not to kill anybody," Ira said.

After that tender scene at juvi I was anxious to see Sophie. She lived in an apartment in North Hollywood, near what they call the NOHO arts district. This was a corridor that was supposed to be pulsating with art, theater, restaurants, clubs. It had at one time been advertised as having a "hip, Millennial, bohemian vibe." Now much of it was shuttered like the rest of the city—restaurants closed, theaters dark, and people moving around with all the joy of Mojave dung beetles.

Sophie's building was two blocks away from a new "tiny homes village." These were 64-square-foot dwellings put up by the city to get the homeless off the streets until they could transition to more permanent housing. The city had no problem moving people in. It was the moving out that was stickier, and of course had demonstrators on both sides of the issue shouting slogans at each other.

At least it was quiet when I picked Sophie up. I buzzed her from the entrance and she said she'd be right out.

I've faced killers with guns and knives. I've been tied up, beaten up, messed up, and fed up. Which is why I couldn't believe how nervous I was waiting for Sophie. A squadron of butterflies did combat exercises in my stomach and chest.

When Sophie came out they went into tailspins.

She was wearing a light gray T-shirt tucked into blue jeans. Casual, but on her it was killer. To top it off she wore a white panama hat, which few people can really rock. She was one of those people.

"Nice day for a drive," I said.

"Let's ride with the top down," she said, and took my arm.

"Spinoza likes that idea," I said.

"I love it that you named your car for a Dutch philosopher."

"I love that you know he was Dutch," I said.

"But why not Aristotle or Socrates?" she asked.

"For one thing, the clever play on words. Spin. That's what we take a car for, right?"

"Ah."

"Spinoza's also challenging, and I like challenges."

"You're something of a challenge yourself, Mike."

"So I've been told."

I opened the passenger door.

Sophie didn't get in. "I like challenges, too," she said.

I should have kissed her then. She was expecting it. But there was something I had to tell her first, and I wasn't ready.

"Duly noted," I said. What a charmer.

She got in.

I got in and started the car. "Where shall we go?"

"I have an idea," Sophie said. "Get on the freeway."

She guided me into Hollywood and then up to Rustic Canyon. She had me pull to a stop where we could overlook the city. The skyline of downtown was so clear you could almost touch it.

"It's a pretty view from up here when the air is clear, isn't it?" Sophie said.

"First time I've been to this spot," I said.

"Not the first time for me." She smiled.

"I am picking up some subtext here."

"Charlie Winkleblack," she said. "He brought me up here the night of our senior prom."

"Dare I ask?"

"Ask what?"

"What transpired between you and Mr. Winkleblack that romantic night."

She laughed. "Mr. Winkleblack happened to be gay. We were in theater together. He was a good friend. We just sat here and looked at the lights and talked about our futures. I was going to UCLA and he was off to CSUN. He wanted to be a Broadway musical star."

"And what did you want to be?"

"I hadn't figured that out yet."

"Not theater?"

"Maybe a little," she said. "After all, I had my big triumph that year. I was Rosalind in *As You Like It*."

"Perfect," I said. "If I were to pick any role you were made for, it would be Rosalind."

"Really?"

"She's the greatest of Shakespeare's heroines. The wittiest, the most gifted. She's the equal of Falstaff, and even better because she's not a fat drunkard."

"Thank you for making that clear."

"And she is unique in that she woos Orlando instead of waiting to be wooed by him."

"Come woo me, woo me, for I am in a holiday humor. What would you say to me now, and I were your very very Rosalind?"

"I would kiss before I spoke," I said.

"You know the lines!"

"Some. It is after all one of the great scenes in Shakespeare."

"So... what *would* you say if I were your very very Rosalind?"

I should have kissed her then, and not spoke.

But I said, "Sophie, I need to tell you something."

She waited.

"You know the work I do," I said.

"Yes."

"Somebody took a shot at me two days ago. With a high-powered rifle."

She stiffened.

"Yeah," I said. "He hit a policeman instead, almost killed him. This was right outside Ira's house. He was waiting for me to show up. And he's still out there."

Sophie looked away from me, out at the city.

"Somebody could ask the question," I said, "why should I do this? Why not move out of L.A. to some quiet burb and get an easy job, like price checker at the 99¢ Store?"

Without moving her head, she said, "What's the answer?"

"For one thing, Ira needs me. I'm his legs and his eyes in places he can't get to. I owe him for saving me from a bad place in my life. He's the only one in this life who cares about me."

"Not the only one," Sophie said.

She put her hand on mine.

I looked at it.

"But there's another thing," I said. "I don't like being pushed. I don't like cutting and running. I don't like leaving the scales unbalanced."

"Scales?"

"Of right and wrong, good and bad. Whenever a bad guy gets away with it an angel loses his wings."

"Who said that?"

"Me," I said. "Just now."

She took her hand away. "Poetic."

"That's why I stay," I said. "Even though there's a cost involved. I don't know if I can ask you to pony up that same cost."

She said, "How about letting me do my own figuring?"

I cleared my throat. "Well, I—"

She touched her finger to my lips. "Pray you, no more of this. 'Tis like the howling of Irish wolves against the moon."

After that we were silent for awhile, looking out at the town. Then we drove around some more. The conversation was light.

But there was heaviness in the silences.

I dropped Sophie back at her place. We said an unsteady goodbye. No touch as she got out. She thanked me for a nice time, but it felt like a kid thanking an aunt for new socks at Christmas. I drove away with a case of German *weltschmerz* filling my chest. That's the weariness you get when you compare the world as it is with your ideal vision of how it should be. I'd allowed myself an ideal vision of Sophie and me, together. Now it was melting away. Leave it to the German philosophers to come up with a word for that. They were not exactly known for their good cheer.

I decided to check on Nick the giant. This would fulfill my duty as assigned by Dr. Artra Murray.

The neighborhood was relatively quiet. I parked across the street and walked up the driveway to the gate. The smell of char was heavy in the air. I looked over the gate and saw the remains of a burned-out garage. Yellow police tape crisscrossed the front of it. Everything inside was black. There was a hole in the roof as if a cannon ball had blasted through.

I went back around to the front door of the house and knocked. Nobody answered. I tried again. Nothing.

When I turned around I saw a boy, maybe eight years old, holding a skateboard and looking right at me.

"I heard it go boom," the boy said.

"You did?" I said.

"Yeah. Boom!"

"Did you know the man who lived there?" I asked.

He nodded. "Nick."

"Do you know where he is now?" I said.

The boy made a slashing motion with his finger across his throat.

I took a step toward him. He backed up.

"I'm not going to hurt you," I said.

"You might give me the virus."

They're sure efficient at pumping fear into the young ones these days.

"I was a friend of his," I said. "Are you saying he's dead?"

Nod.

"When did this happen?"

"Um... yesterday night."

"Are you sure he's dead?"

"My mom said."

"Is your mom home?"

He nodded.

"I'd like to talk to her. Would that be okay?"

He looked at the ground.

"Can you take me to your house?"

"Um..."

"I'll stay far away so I don't give anybody the virus."

"Um..."

"What's your name?"

"Cyrus."

"Mine's Mike. I really want to know what happened."

"There was a fire."

"Right." We had reached a cul-de-sac in our conversa-tion. Which was why I was happy to see the nervous-looking woman coming toward us calling, "Cyrus! Come on home, honey."

The boy started toward her.

"Are you his mother?" I said.

"Who are you?" she said.

"A friend of Nick's," I said. "I was visiting here just a couple of days ago. Can you tell me what happened?"

Suspicion lined her eyes, and who could blame her? This is the city, the fear of strangers has amped up, and I'm not exactly the cuddly type to begin with.

But she softened, and said. "There was an explosion. It knocked some dishes out of my cabinet. When we came out to see it was on fire."

"Was it a bomb?"

"It sounded like it. But I know he used to cook in there and he wasn't supposed to."

"Do you know what they did with the body?"

"I'm sorry, no," she said. "You could ask John."

"John?"

"He lives here."

I remembered Nick telling me it was an ex-con who rented the garage to him.

"Thanks," I said.

The woman started to walk away, holding the boy's hand.

Cyrus looked back at me and said, "Bye."

"Bye," I said.

I went to a front window and peeked in through the curtain crack. No lights on.

I called Ira.

"That guy I knocked out in my flower garden. His place burned down, and he was apparently inside when it happened."

"His whole house?" Ira said.

"He lived in the garage in back. There was an explosion. A neighbor thinks it might have been some sort of cooking accident."

"Like propane, perhaps?"

"He did have a Coleman stove," I said. "I don't think that'd be enough for what happened."

"Incendiary device, perhaps," Ira said. "Any investigators on scene?"

"Not at the moment," I said.

"I'll see what I can find out," Ira said.

"Can you track the body?"

"It will be under the jurisdiction of the county coroner, and any suspicious or violent death is subject to investigation. I know someone in the office."

"Thanks," I said.

"What are you going to do now?"

"Some reading," I said. "And wait for the landlord to show up."

. . .

It took an hour for him to show. He drove a Ford pickup and parked in the driveway. He was about six feet tall, buzzed hair, wearing a T-shirt, black jeans and black boots. The clothes all seemed crisp and clean. He wasn't coming from a work site. As he walked toward the front door he leafed through some mail.

I got out of Spinoza. "John?"

He looked at me. His face was not unappealing. While there was a studied ex-con look about him, his blue eyes were of the light variety that women love.

But those eyes were suspicious as I approached.

"I knew Nick," I said.

He looked me up and down. "Romeo?"

"That's me."

"Come on inside."

The decor was not what I expected. The furniture looked new. On the wall above the sofa was a big, framed photograph of John, shirtless, wearing loose cotton slacks and a mirthless expression. On the bottom right, in fancy script, it said Dolce & Gabbana.

"I don't think that's a selfie," I said.

John tossed his mail on the coffee table. "Not bad, huh?"

"Dolce & Gabbana, huh?"

"I'm getting into modeling."

"Your PO get you that?"

He laughed. "Nah, I got it all on my own, with the help of a fine lady. Funny who you meet in this town. You could be having a hamburger and some chick from a modeling agency sees you and there you go."

"You're Lana Turner," I said.

"What?"

"Lana Turner, the actress."

He shook his head.

"From the old Hollywood days," I said. "When she was a teenager she was sitting at a drugstore in Hollywood, wearing a tight sweater, and she got noticed by a studio scout. She became a big movie star."

"See what I mean?" John said.

"Let me ask you about the explosion."

"Happened around eleven last night."

"Must have knocked you out of bed."

He smiled. "No way. I was in bed, but not here."

"I get it."

"It's a crime scene and they're going to send a specialized team. Really sucks what happened."

"Think it was a bomb?"

"I have no idea," he said.

"Think it might have been a cooking accident?"

"Again, no idea. Nick told me about you. You did a real paint job on his face."

"I'm sure he told you he wanted to do the same thing to me."

"Something like that," John said.

"Are you the one who hooked him up with San Dae-Ho?"

Stiffening, John said, "Is that any of your business?"

"Yes."

"Why?"

"How often have you worked with Dae-Ho?"

"Got nothing to do with him. Don't want nothing to do with him. That's as far as it goes."

"I'm not satisfied," I said.

"I don't care," John said.

"Maybe your modeling agency would care," I said.

He started a stare down. It's a prison thing.

I kept a poker face. "They might be interested in people who refer leg breakers who later get blown up on their property."

"I already told you, I wasn't here."

"You didn't have to be."

The fashion model went calmly to a shelf with a black box on it. He opened the box and pulled out 9 mm automatic.

"Get out," he said.

"Like you're going to shoot me and put at risk all that modeling jack."

"I told you I didn't have anything to do with Nick's death, okay?"

"I believe in the presumption of innocence," I said. "But I also gather evidence. And I'm asking you about San Dae-Ho."

After a pause he put the gun back in the box.

"Sit down," he said.

I took a chair and he took the sofa.

"I know about Dae-Ho. He was here once. He's not somebody I ever want to see again. I don't know what he and Nick had worked out. I'm legit now, and want to stay that way. I'm bummed about Nick."

"Have you talked to the police?"

"I got a phone call. They're sending somebody out tonight. I'm going to cooperate in any way I can."

"How about Nick's next of kin?"

"I think he has a brother. I don't know anyone else."

"I don't suppose you know how to get hold of the brother."

John shook his head.

"Your uncle owns this place?" I asked.

"Yeah."

"Where is he?"

"New Mexico."

"He have a record?"

"What's the point of all this?"

"I just ask questions," I said.

"That's all I'm going to say," John said. "I'll save anything else for the cops."

"Need a lawyer?"

"Absolutely not."

I gave him one of Ira's cards. "Just in case," I said. "And if you hear anything, I'd appreciate you letting us know."

"I want to know what happened, same as you," John said.

Maybe. But I wasn't ruling him out for complicity in Nick's death.

B ack at my palatial room at the Motel 6, I called Ira and filled him in on my interview with John.

Ira told me the D.A. was taking Clint's case to a new and lower level.

"Meaning what?" I asked.

"Get this," Ira said. "They're going to argue that his suicide attempt demonstrates consciousness of guilt."

"Say what?"

"There's a California Jury Instruction, number 372 to be exact. It says if a defendant fled or tried to flee immediately after the crime or after being accused of the crime, the jury may take this into account as demonstrating consciousness of guilt."

"I don't see the relevance."

"They're going to argue that when Clint attempted suicide, he was trying to flee life."

"You have got to be kidding."

"Wish I was," Ira said.

"They can't be serious."

"And yet they are."

"Don't words have meaning anymore?" I said.

"Post-modernism and political correctness are a witch's brew, Michael. Words mean only what people want them to mean, and only then as a means to power."

"Humpty-Dumptyism," I said.

"Precisely," Ira said.

We were referring to the bit from Lewis Carroll's *Through the Looking-Glass.*

"When I use a word," Humpty Dumpty said, in rather a scornful tone, "it means just what I choose it to mean—neither more nor less."

"The question is," said Alice, "whether you can make words mean so many different things."

"The question is," said Humpty Dumpty, "which is to be master —that's all."

"Ol' Humpty saw it coming, didn't he?" I said.

"Where are you now, Michael?"

"At a Motel 6 in the Valley."

"Your hideout?"

"I prefer to think of it as a lovely garden spot."

"Is there a garden?"

"No," I said. "But words mean what I choose them to mean."

"You can come over here, you know."

"You don't need the added worry," I said.

"I worry about you anyway, Michael."

"I know you do."

"That includes your soul."

"I know it does."

"Let's keep working on it," Ira said.

"I love you, too," I said.

.   .   .

The sirens are lovely at night in the Valley, and the police helicopters like whippoorwills singing their plaintive song.

Folklore holds that whippoorwills singing near a house are an omen of death or bad luck.

Great.

I did fifty push-ups and fifty crunches, then spread out on the floor looking up at the ceiling. I thought of Sophie and how she seemed to be floating away from me. In one sense I was glad about it, for her sake. In another sense, I was sick about it, for my sake. The ceiling offered no solace.

So I went over questions in my mind. Like, who took a shot at me? How did Nick die? Where did this San Dae-Ho clown fit into things?

Who was running the drug trade at Elias and using Clint Cunningham as a dealer?

What did TBD mean in Clint's drawing?

"So what do you have for me?" I asked the ceiling.

Got no answer. I considered the French existentialists who believe there *is* no answer. Life is absurd. It's all waiting for Godot, who never shows up.

There's something inside me that resists surrendering to absurdity.

On the other hand, I was talking to a motel ceiling.

The next morning it was Sunday in L.A., a strange time in the city. People going to church or Costco, to the beach or the mountains. Or they stay at home—many with fear o' the virus—and watch golf or football, cooking shows or shopping networks. No one does serious business, so all the important matters are on hold.

I gave C Dog a call to remind him that tonight was the

night he was going drug buying in Hollywood. He said, "I'm ready, Eddie."

I walked to a Burger King and got myself a fine break-fast—if one can say that without being oxymoronic. It had sourdough bread, something yellow that might have been an egg, and a sausage patty with cheese on it.

I was ready to take on the world after that.

Or not.

Nothing against Burger King. It serves a purpose. It makes an acceptable breakfast sandwich and a pretty good hamburger. Just not the best in the world. That honor belonged to a little place called Nell's a few blocks from my prep school. It was where my mother brought me one time when Dad was at Oxford delivering a paper on the phenom-enology of Edmund Husserl.

It was the day when one of my classmates pushed my face into a mud puddle.

I was very quiet at home. So for dinner Mom took me to Nell's. She knew I loved it. It cooked the fattest, tastiest burgers in New Haven. Heck, probably all of New England. And though she would have preferred I have a healthy soup or salad, she knew this day was not one to force those upon me.

We sat at a table on the sidewalk.

"You've had it rough," Mom said.

I only nodded, and took a bite of my comfort.

"This should come as no surprise, Michael. You've been given a gift, a rare mind, and that is going to trigger the human weakness of envy."

I nodded.

"This will come out in ways that hurt," she said. "Very deeply sometimes. There are three ways you can react. You can withdraw, attack, or repose. Knowing you as I do, I suspect your first instinct is to withdraw. You get silent."

I said nothing.

"You don't want to be with people, even people your own age. Being at school with older kids is not easy. But that is a crucible for your gift, Michael, and you will come out of it stronger, and better, and will contribute good things in this life."

I tried to believe her.

"Some people go on the attack," she said. "I'm glad that is not your choice. Which leaves us with repose. Do you know what I mean by that?"

"Rest," I said.

"Not only that. It means to quietly give attention to the formation of your soul. It means attending to your emotions, but not letting emotions be your master. Your emotions matter, but as an ambiance. Your mind—your gift —directs you in this."

My hamburger was half done.

"There's a verse in the Bible," Mom said. "In quietness and in trust will be your strength."

"Trust what?" I said.

"Who do you think?"

"Who?"

She smiled at me.

"God, of course," I said.

"That's what repose means," she said.

Then she reached across the table and put her hand on my cheek. It was the softest, loveliest, most comforting touch I've ever felt.

I started to cry.

She moved her chair around next to mine and put her arm around my shoulder.

I was embarrassed, being out on the street like that, with tears. But my mother being there made it all right.

At that moment I started to trust.

But all that blew up when my mother and father were murdered, leaving me alone in the world. So what did I do? I withdrew. Developed a nice, thick ice ring.

And then I started to attack.

As arranged, C Dog met me at the motel. He was dressed for the part—floppy black T-shirt with *Punk's Not Dead* emblazoned across it, low-riding blue jeans, battered black Converse high tops. Then again, that's how he usually dressed.

We drove into Hollywood separately and parked in the cavernous garage at Hollywood and Highland.

I went out first, walking a block to something called The Museum of Illusions. This is where you can go in with your girlfriend and get your picture taken of the two of you on a raft with the sinking Titanic in the background. Perfect visual metaphor for our times. And it'll only set you back sixty bucks.

Outside there's an alcove doorway. That's where I set up so I could view the Scientology building across the street. Originally, it was the Christie Hotel, which opened in 1922 as Hollywood's first high-rise. It's one of several Hollywood landmarks Scientology has gobbled up over the decades.

As I waited for C Dog to show, a bit of Hollywood Boulevard enterprise unfolded in front of me. A guy about fifty or so with gray hair and jeans came along, carrying a big white bucket and a sign. He turned the bucket over and sat on it. He put a plastic bowl down in front of him, fished out a bill from his pocket and threw it in the bowl. Then he lit a cigarette and put up the sign for all to see. In hand lettering it said *Need Money for Hookers and Coke.*

He gave me a quick glance. He had the look of a dog who had just peed on the carpet.

Coincidentally, that's exactly how I saw him.

Thirty seconds later a man and woman—who looked like they'd stepped off the Greyhound from Wichita—stopped and gawked. Then laughed. The guy on the bucket gave them a fifty-watt smile.

The man took out his phone and said, "Tricia has got to see this!"

The bucket guy gave him a thumbs-up.

The man took a picture. And started to walk away.

The bucket guy said, "*Ahem!*"

Mr. and Mrs. Wichita turned around.

Bucket Guy pointed to the bowl.

"Oh!" Mr. Wichita said, recognizing his egregious faux pas. He quickly snatched a buck from his wallet and dropped it in the bowl.

"Have a nice evening," said Bucket Guy. Then he looked at me again. Now he had triumph in his eyes. I still pictured him as that dog.

He said, "Is this a great country or what?"

"It's a privilege to watch you," I said.

"Hey, I'm not robbing anybody." He frowned and took a drag on his cig.

I folded my arms and looked up the street. C Dog was crossing Highland. He had a nice, lost-looking shuffle going. The kid had talent.

Except when he broke the fourth wall. After slow walking past the Scientology building, he gave me a quick look, and shrugged.

I balled my fists and turned my back, hoping he got the message.

"What's the matter with you?" Bucket Guy said.

Turning around, I relaxed my hands and thought about moving to another location. I decided Bucket Guy was the perfect pawn in my chess game. If I was in conversation with him it wouldn't look so much like I was casing the scene.

So I slid down to a sitting position. This is not an uncommon look on Hollywood Boulevard. From here I could look at Bucket Guy and still watch the Scientology building. C Dog stood on the corner, looking around, and not anymore at me.

"How long have you been running this scam?" I said.

"This is no scam," he said.

"No?"

"Why do you even care?"

"I like to study human nature," I said.

"Yeah, right," Bucket Guy said. "You're just floating through life studying human nature, la-dee-dah."

"Nobody floats through life," I said. "You sink or swim."

"There you go. This is me swimming. I'm not making anybody unhappy. I'm providing people with some laughs. They give me some money. Where's the harm in that?"

"When you put it that way—"

"I mean, I could be out there holding people up with a gun."

"You have a point."

"I tried working, but I don't like it. So I come down here and take in some funds, tax free. I'm an entertainer. It's what I've always wanted to do anyway."

I glanced across the street and saw C Dog doing his aimless act. He had his hands in his pockets, and was walking in little circles.

"Originally," Bucket Guy said, "I thought I'd be a standup comedian and maybe get my own series, like Jerry Seinfeld. Or a talk show. That didn't work out. I did some sales in a boiler room. And you know what? You lie all the time. You work the phone and the emails with a script that tells how your store went out of business and you have to move all this merch. I didn't like lying to people, so I figured, why not tell the truth? I tried a sign that said 'Just need money to live on.' You know what that got me? Bupkis. So that's when I came up with something brilliant. A lie that is obvious entertainment, which means it's no lie at all."

"You're a philosopher."

"A businessman. If you can make 'em laugh, they'll give you the dough. Capitalism!"

As if on cue, a couple of young women stopped and giggled. Bucket Guy put on his entertainer face and smiled. One of the women turned to me and said, "Would you take our picture?"

Never one to turn down a reasonable request, I stood and took the phone she handed me. They got on either side of Bucket Guy and everybody smiled. I took the shot.

"Don't forget to feed the kitty," I said, handing back the phone.

The women looked perplexed.

"He's here to make a living," I said.

"Oh yeah," said the one with the phone. "Give him something."

The other woman fed a dollar into the cap, and the two moved on.

"Thanks," Bucket Guy said.

"Doing my part for the free market," I said.

Across the street, a guy walked up to C Dog and started talking. C Dog listened, nodded. The guy turned and C Dog followed. They disappeared around the corner.

"Who are you really?" Bucket Guy said.

I stood. "Gotta go."

"Aw, we were just getting started. I get a little lonely out here."

"If I meet a talent scout from NBC, I'll send him your way."

"Deal!"

I walked to the corner and saw C Dog and the mad hatter huddled on the side street. The exchange was quick. C Dog, as I'd instructed, walked back toward Highland. The hatter continued further on down the side street, crossed over, and turned into a fenced area. I figured it to be a parking lot of some sort.

A few minutes later the hatter came walking back to the boulevard, and took up residence there once more.

I crossed the street.

H alfway down the side street I saw him. He was leaning on a black Caddie, counting some bills. He wore a white sport jacket with the sleeves pushed up to the elbows, black pants, white shoes. His hair was dark and slicked back in a manner that made him look like Lucifer or a governor of California.

"Danny Durant?" I said.

His head jerked up. He looked surprised for a second, then tried to cover it with street bravado. All these expressions look the same—the head lolls back on the neck, the mouth drops open a little, the eyes narrow.

He stuffed the money in the pocket of his jacket. "Who?"

"Danny, short for Daniel. Durant. That would be you."

"And you're a cop," he said. A good move on his part. There's nothing preventing a cop from lying about his status, but even low-life street scum can usually tell when he is.

"I'm just an interested third party," I said.

"So?"

"What I mean is," I said, "I'm interested in what you're doing at Elias."

"Elias?"

"You're one of its illustrious graduates, right?"

"Get lost."

"Work with me, Danny."

He paused a moment, smiled. "Don't think I will."

The change in his demeanor told me we were not alone. Sure enough, a guy from the streetside was walking toward us. Big and wide. Another ex-con type. He wore a military jacket. His hands were in the pockets. He withdrew his right and showed me his knuckledusters—hard plastic. They don't trigger metal detectors like their brass cousins, but can do just as much damage to a skull. The right blow can send you to the big sleep.

"Time to go," Danny Durant said.

Knuckleduster rotated his fist a couple of times.

"It doesn't have to be like this," I said. "I only have a couple of questions. Very civilized."

"You see my man?" Danny Durant said. "Don't mess with my man. He kills. And he likes it."

That seemed to describe him perfectly.

I back-fisted Danny in the face. He screamed and grabbed his newly broken nose.

Knuckleduster charged.

T he French martial art of kickboxing—known as *savate* —developed out of street fighting in Paris and Marseille back in the eighteenth century. It comes from the French word for "old boot," which is what their soldiers and sailors wore. That boot could do damage when delivered to the right spot on an opponent.

As far as I know, there is no French word for "deadly tennis shoe." Nor is there a martial art associated with sneakers. But I am not a founder of any fighting school other than *Do it to him before he does it to you.*

I jumped, my body perpendicular to the ground, and smashed Knuckleduster in the gut with my left shoe.

He doubled over.

I popped both sides of his head with my cupped hands, blasting his eardrums and disabling his equilibrium. Then I gave him Romeo's Hammer, a right to the temple, sending him to the ground.

I stomped his right wrist, bent over and took off the plastic knuckles. His mouth was open wide, sucking for air. I stuck the plastic knuckles in his mouth and shoved. He made guttural noises, like a man drowning inside a cement mixer.

When I looked up, Danny Durant was in his Caddie.

The car gunned forward. But it had to make a wide turn to get out of the lot.

Which gave me the opportunity to Gretzky him. The great Wayne Gretzky once explained, "I don't go to where the puck is. I go to where the puck is going to be."

I ran to where his car was going to be.

The heel is the most underrated part of the human anatomy. For example, it is the only way to kick in a door. All those cops on TV using front kicks would only end up with a dislocated hip. Or worse, using their shoulders on a door would get them only broken clavicles. A mule kick is the only way to do it.

And to smash the glass of a car window, the well-placed heel is a natural ball-peen hammer.

Just before he got to the driveway of the little lot I jumped and heeled the window.

The glass shattered. Danny drove his car into an iron post.

H e was a little muddled.

I punched his face through the window. He got more muddled. I reached in and opened the door and dragged him out by his coat.

Knuckleduster was still groaning on the ground. Holding Durant with one hand, I went over and gave Knuckleduster a kick to the side of the head, enough to keep him down for awhile longer.

I walked Durant around the car. It was like helping a drunk to a cab. I opened the passenger door and shoved him in the seat. His chin hit his chest, which was stained with the blood pouring from his nose.

I got in the driver's side, backed up, and drove out of the lot.

Durant moaned as I drove several blocks until I found a relatively quiet zone. I parked at the curb.

"How you feeling?" I said.

In a wheezy voice Durant said, "What're you gonna do?"

I grabbed a hunk of his thick, sticky hair and jerked his head up.

"I'm going to give you a chance to live," I said.

His eyes fluttered. "Whu?"

I turned his head toward me, like a ventriloquist's dummy. "You've got one chance. Tell me about your operation at Elias. All of it."

"I told you, I don't know."

"Wrong answer." I squeezed the hair in my fist.

"Stop!"

"Goodbye, Danny."

"Wait, wait, wait!" His eyes were as big as tires now. "I used to. But not anymore. Not for a couple years."

"You moved on to greener pastures?"

"Yeah."

"Why?"

When he didn't answer, I put my left hand hard on his neck and began to squeeze.

"Wait!"

"Hurry it up," I said.

"I got told to back off," Danny said.

"Who told you?"

"I don't know. I just know..."

"Go on."

"They killed my dog."

I let go of him.

He tried to breathe in deep. He touched his nose with the back of his hand. "You broke it."

"I want a name, a lead. Anything. I want to find out who's trafficking at Elias. You know more than you're telling me."

"I just want to be left alone, you know? I got another territory."

"You and your enforcer."

"So what?"

"You're a drug dealer, Danny. You know how low on the scum ladder that is?"

"You're not a cop, what do you care?"

"No man is an island."

"What the... what does that even mean?"

"It's from a poem. It means any man's death diminishes me, because I am involved in mankind."

His look was uncomprehending. Thanks, public schooling.

"Here's what I mean," I said. "I don't like what you do. It's a net negative in life. We've got enough negatives. If I kill you, it will move the needle the other way, toward the positive. That's the way I'm leaning now."

"Oh, man, come on—"

"So you give me a lead, and make it a good one, because I know how to find you."

"Please, don't."

"A name," I said.

"I don't know!"

I moved my hand back to his throat.

"Wait!" he said. "Let me think."

"You do that."

"I can't think with your hand there."

I took my hand away.

He breathed in and out a couple of times. "Look," he said, "the only name I can think of is Shibuk."

"That's a name?"

"Yeah."

"First or last?"

"I don't know. I only know Shibuk."

"How do you spell it?"

"How should I know?"

"Who is this guy?" I said.

"Some kind of accountant. A numbers guy. He might know about Elias."

"Why?"

"He's connected, that's all I know. Out in the Valley."

"That's it? That's all you've got for me?"

"You gotta believe me."

"Why do I gotta? You're a scum."

"Quit saying that."

"Scum."

"That's all I know. I swear."

"Your swearing does not carry any weight," I said. "But for some odd reason I believe you."

His body visibly relaxed. "Thank you, man."

"Now you can thank me for saving your soul."

"Huh?"

"You're out of the drug business," I said.

"Wait, what?"

"I don't want to find out that you're peddling dust, or anything else."

His mouth opened. No words came out.

"If I find out otherwise," I said, "I'm going to track you down and this time there won't be any talking. Instead, I'll gut you like a haddock. Have you ever seen a gutted haddock?"

A slow shake of the head.

"Guts all over the place," I said. "You step on them and slide all over. Really, it's quite unattractive. Am I getting through to you?"

"I don't know anything anymore. Look at me. Look at my car."

"No, you look at me. You see the severity in my look?"

"The what?"

"Severity."

"What the h—"

"It means very serious, and in a very bad way."

"All right. You told me."

"But I don't get the feeling you believe me."

"Oh man, just let me go now."

"All right, Danny."

"Thank you."

"Just one more thing."

I almost felt bad doing it. Almost. I gave him a left fist to the zygoma, otherwise known as the cheekbone. He slumped, his head thunking against the window. He would be out for some time, at least long enough for me to walk back to get my car.

I drove back to the motel where C Dog was waiting for me leaning on his car.

"Did you see that?" he said, arms out wide. "Was I great or what?"

"A regular Brando," I said.

"A what?"

"A *who*. Brando. The actor."

He shook his head.

"I forgot," I said. "Your movie knowledge begins with *Shrek*."

"Shrek is cool."

"You were a regular Shrek."

"Thanks, man," C Dog said.

"Aren't you forgetting something?"

"What? Oh!" He took a little plastic baggie out of his pocket and handed it to me.

"What're you gonna do with it?" he asked.

"Take it to the police."

"Why don't you just flush it down the toilet?" he said.

"You want all those alligators in the sewer to get high on this stuff?"

"There's alligators down there?"

"We're going to do this legally," I said.

"I'm cool with that."

I put my hand on his shoulder. "You have done well, Doggerel. You may return to your domicile and sleep well. And dream of lions."

He beamed.

· · ·

B ack in my room I called Ira and, as usual, made my confession.

"Was that really necessary?" Ira said. "Wait, don't answer that. I already know what you're going to say."

"At least I got something," I said. "A name. Shibuk. S-H-I-B-U-K, I'm thinking. Some kind of criminal accountant. Turn your skills toward finding him."

"Do you have a clue in what haystack this needle might be located?"

"Maybe the Valley."

"Ah, that narrows it down."

"Happy to help."

Pause.

"How do you feel, Michael?"

"Feel? Okay."

"No. Really. Because every time you go through something like this it affects you, and I need to know how."

"Why?"

"This may come as a shock. Because I care about you."

"I'll be fine."

Pause.

Ira said, "Will you at least stay calm?"

"Of course. I'm a laid back kind of guy."

I think I heard a snort.

B ut Ira was right, as he usually is. I was not feeling okay. I took a walk and went into a liquor store and bought a six-pack of Corona and a packaged burrito. I came back to my room, turned on the TV news, and cooked the burrito in the microwave.

Living the dream.

The burrito tasted like an old paperback. The beer was necessary to wash it down.

The news was not helpful for anything.

A six-year-old boy had been shot and killed in a road rage incident in Orange. His mother was driving on the freeway and a guy in a white sedan cut her off. She laid on the horn. The guy changed lanes, slowed, and came up behind her, and fired two shots. One of them killed the boy. Police put out the word for anyone who might have seen the incident to get hold of them.

At a tony restaurant in Beverly Hills, five masked men shouting anti-semitic slurs burst in and started spraying diners with mace. Two men in yarmulkes having dinner with their wives were dragged off and beaten. The attackers took off and have not been found.

But the weather was nice! The TV weatherman—I mean "meteorologist"—flicked his hand up and down in front of the green screen, showing mild temperatures throughout the Los Angeles basin. His smile was wide and his teeth so white they burned my retinas.

When they announced an upcoming story on Prince Harry and Meghan Markle, I forced the last of the burrito down my throat and turned the thing off.

For a moment there was silence in my room. No sirens or choppers or honking horns.

All the noise was in my head.

I couldn't stop thinking about the six-year-old boy.

Next morning I showered, shaved and treated myself to a real breakfast at Las Fuentes, an authentic Mexican restaurant in Reseda. I ordered *huevos rancheros* and ate them at an outdoor table, where I had a view of the auto body shop across the street.

What looked like a mourning dove flapped down onto the railing near my table. It gave me the side-eye. Or maybe it was looking at the flour tortilla I'd just filled with beans and rice. I tore off a small bit of tortilla and tossed it onto the empty table next to me. The dove winged over, picked up the fragment in its beak, and flew off.

Feeling at one with nature, I finished my meal and allowed myself a few minutes of sated satisfaction before returning to the world of men.

First order of business was calling Shane McGuane's talent agency.

A pleasant female voice answered. "Barkley-McClellan."

"I'd like to speak to Shane McGuane, please."

"This is Mr. McGuane's agency."

"Right," I said.

"He does not take personal calls here," she said.

"Then just give me his phone number."

"We certainly cannot do that. May I ask what this is regarding?"

"Publicity," I said.

"Are you with a PR firm?"

"I work alone."

"If you'd like to leave your name and number..."

"I'd rather you get a message to Mr. McGuane. Can you do that for me?"

"I can put you through to Mr. Barkley's assistant. Please hold."

I held.

"Mr. Barkley's office," said a man's soft voice.

"Hi there," I said. "I was told you're the one to talk to. I've got a very important message for your client, Shane McGuane, one that he will definitely want to hear. Can I give it to you?"

"What is the message?"

"Tell him I'm the guy he met at Tab's Hot Dogs the

other day, and I think I can keep the bad publicity from getting out there."

"Excuse me, did you say bad publicity?"

"He'll understand. Give him my number and tell him to call me sometime today so we can straighten things out."

"Um... can I place you on hold for a moment?"

"Only a moment," I said.

Some music came on that sounded like a Bernard Herrmann score from a Hitchcock movie. Good choice for being on hold with a Hollywood agent.

A minute later a man's voice snapped, "Who is this?"

"You first," I said.

"Milt Barkley, I'm Shane's agent. Who are you?"

"My name's Romeo."

"Sure it is."

"First name Mike."

"Sounds fake."

"You can call me Justin Bieber if you like."

"What's this about bad publicity? And hurry it up."

"Shane can give you the details. I tried to have a decent conversation with him the other day at Tab's Hot Dogs. I'm an investigator for an attorney here in town."

"What are you investigating Shane for?"

"Not Shane. His son goes to school with a client of ours, and I needed to get some information. Shane was not forthcoming, and unleashed a couple of his stuntmen friends on me."

He said, "You threatening a lawsuit?"

"Not at all," I said. "I just want to talk to Shane. Nothing more."

"What if he doesn't want to talk to you?"

"Then maybe I'll file a lawsuit."

F-words started flying out of his mouth. He went on a rant telling me what I could do with my lawsuit and how he'd bury me in lawyers and if I knew what was good for me I would never contact Shane or Barkley-McClellan or—

"Drugs," I said.

Pause.

"Drugs and kids," I said. "How would you like a story like that planted in the trades?"

Silence.

"You're weighing costs right now, Mr. Barkley. Otherwise, you would have hung up on me. You know you're not going to follow through because this is precisely the thing Shane needs to avoid, and you want him to avoid, if you ever hope to recoup your investment in him. How'm I doing so far?"

He didn't answer.

"Good," I said. "And the price for keeping things on a nice, even keel is a small one, just encouraging Shane to have a talk with me, and that'll be the end of it. Why don't you talk it over with him and have him give me a call?"

Pause.

"What's your number?"

I gave it to him.

He said, "But if you threaten any trouble after this, I will unleash holy hell on you."

"I believe you are sincere," I said.

"I am."

"Which makes you the exception."

"The what?"

"My grandfather told me about the old time radio comedian Fred Allen. He once said, 'You can take all the sincerity in Hollywood and put it into a gnat's navel, and still have room for two caraway seeds and an agent's heart.'"

Pause.

"You're really a legit investigator?" he asked.

"Authorized and approved."

"You ever do freelance work?"

"Seldom."

"It might be worth both our whiles to have a meeting sometime."

"It's funny how our relationship has changed," I said.

"This is Hollywood, my friend. Things move fast. Give me a call."

"And we'll do lunch?" I said.

"Of course," he said.

"I'd appreciate your getting my message to Shane."

"It'll be done." He then reminded me that if I effed with him holy hell would be unleashed upon me.

I went back inside Las Fuentes and refilled my coffee. I came out again and saw the mourning dove pecking away at my crumbs. I sat and put my feet up on another chair and watched a tow truck pull into the auto body shop with a sad-looking Corvette. Half the car's hood was gone, the other half smashed into a V shape.

Fifteen minutes later Shane called.

"I don't appreciate this at all," he said.

"Let's talk about it."

"I can't believe you called my agent."

"How else could I get to you?"

"You could sneak up on me when I'm eating."

"Now you can do the same to me," I said. "I'm outside at Las Fuentes. You know it?"

"Sure," he said.

"I thought this would be a good place to talk."

"You want to talk in person?" he said.

"Yep. And only to you, not your buddies."

"Why should I?"

I said, "I went over all this with your agent. A sharp

blade, that Mr. Barkley. It'll be a relatively painless fifteen minutes or so. I'll even buy you breakfast."

"I ate," he said.

"Coffee then," I said.

"Fine," he said.

Twenty minutes later he showed.

"Thanks for coming," I said.

"Can we get this over with?" he said.

"Have a seat. Take anything in your coffee?"

"Black," he said.

I went in and got him a coffee and came back and set it on the table. He was looking at his phone.

"Unbelievable," he said.

"What is?" I said.

"People are bat crazy."

"That's entirely believable."

"Fear porn," he said. "They want us to be afraid forever, like little gerbils."

"Good image," I said.

He put his phone down. "I gotta be careful what I say."

"Oh?"

"Hollywood's a small town. Say the wrong thing and you're toast. Think the wrong thing, and you're burnt toast."

"Really? I thought Hollywood was a vast, verdant meadow of free thought and the rational exchange of ideas."

Shane McGuane smiled. "You might be okay."

"Let's not be hasty," I said. "Tell me about your relation-ship with Gavin."

"It's fine," he said.

"How much time does he spend with you?"

"Why does this matter?"

"Humor me."

"When he wants to, he comes over."

"When he wants to?"

"He prefers living with his mother."

"She has a nice house."

"Courtesy of me, thank you very much. Part of the settlement, only..."

I waited. He gripped his coffee cup like he wanted to break it.

He said, "It's a hell of a thing, having an ex who makes more money than you do, after she took you to the cleaners."

"She does pretty well, does she?"

"You met her, right?"

"Right."

"She's one of those top producers. She never lets an opportunity go by to remind me of that."

I nodded.

"Let me tell you," he said, and leaned forward like it was important. "There was some domestic abuse, okay? I don't like to admit it."

"Were you ever charged?"

"Not me! Her! She was the one who laid it on. There was a time when I was sleeping and she smashed my head with a book! You know how that hurts?"

Thinking of Sammie Sand, I said, "I have an idea, yes."

"Another time she turned on me with a frying pan full of bacon and threw the whole thing at me. She's crazy."

"That sounds like reason enough for divorce."

Bitterness bent his mouth. "What was that old country song? She got the gold mine and I got the shaft."

He sat back and got a faraway look.

"You know," he said, "there was a time they compared

me to James Dean. The critics. Said I had the magnetism. Can you imagine that?"

"I can see it."

"Thanks for saying so. But that was then. It only takes a flop and crazy ex-wife to turn magnetism into sh—"

"I get it. And hard times follow."

"A comeback is a long, hard road," he said. His look was pleading. "I can't have anything go wrong."

"I'm not interested in anything going wrong," I said.

"But what does any of this have to do with Gavin?"

"Who bought Gavin his car?"

"His mother. Why?"

"Just checking. Does Gavin do drugs?"

Shane McGuane shook his head. "Nothing outside some weed like everybody else."

"Do you really think your ex is supporting her lifestyle on what she makes as an agent?"

"Why wouldn't I think that?"

"Just asking."

"She's good at what she does, which is flinging bull—" He stopped himself, thought about it. "You know, that's part of it, isn't it?"

"What is?"

"Lying. You've got to be a pretty good liar to sell things."

"Not always," I said.

"Call it tweaking the truth then," he said. "That's what you do as an actor, right? That's what you do when you sell."

"Do you think she's capable of covering a great, big lie?" I said.

"Like what?"

"She likes money," I said. "She needs money. Maybe she gets it all from real estate. But then again, maybe there's something else going on. And maybe she's got Gavin involved."

He sat up straight. "Involved in what?"

"Selling drugs at Elias."

If a face can drain of color, his did. "What evidence do you have of that?"

"I had a talk with Gavin and his girlfriend on Friday."

"Where?"

"At a park. Gavin knew something about drug dealing at Elias. He denied he was into it, and put me on to a guy. But that could have been a lie."

Shane McGuane frowned.

I said, "You could be lying, too."

That hit him like a slap. "Is that what this is about? You brought me here to accuse me? Accuse my kid?"

"Just asking questions."

"That stinks. You butt into people's lives. You don't care what you say."

"Maybe I care more than you think."

"About what?"

"Truth."

"Sure," he said. "We done?"

"I'll give you the last shot," I said. "Do you think your boy or your ex might in some way be involved in dealing, even at a low level?"

"I don't know anything anymore," he said. "Who does?"

He looked like he wanted to say more, so I waited.

He sighed. "When I married Mandi I was the hot one, the one with all the money and potential. She didn't even have her license then. After Gavin came along she was a good mom for awhile, but got antsy. Wanted to do something on her own. Started cheating on me."

"Did you ever cheat on her?"

"No. I did not. I can tell you that face-to-face. And I could have. I had lots of opportunity."

"Is she seeing anyone now?"

"I'm sure she is. I just don't know who."

"Suppose I wanted to find out," I said.

"You kidding?"

"Why would I kid?"

He drank the last of his coffee, then said, "I don't think you'd have a problem, if you put some effort into it. She's, what's the word..."

"Insatiable?"

"What's that mean?"

"An appetite that isn't satisfied."

He pointed at me. "That's it!"

We left it there. I got back in my car feeling a little nauseous. Not because of the food, but at the prospect of acting like a run-of-the-mill shamus looking for evidence of infidelity.

I called Ira.

"I'm a window peeper now," I said.

"What are you talking about?"

I explained.

"Is that the best use of your time?" Ira said.

"What else have I got?" I said. "I have to run down every lead in this thing."

"Well, there's another item to consider. My contact at the coroner's office had a very interesting bit of news about your friend Nick. The presumed cause of death is smoke inhalation. The body is badly burned. But they did find a sign of trauma to the trachea."

"Meaning he could have been strangled."

"Exactly."

"Great. Something more to think about as I wait to testify."

"Ah, the preliminary hearing for Sammie Sand."

"Tomorrow."

"Do you want me to give you a little coaching?"

"How much sarcasm will it remove from me?"

"Hopefully, all of it."

"Then no, I'm good."

"Michael—"

"Kidding. I'll be my soft, respectful self."

"What I'm afraid of," Ira said.

W hen I got back at the motel I took a beer out to the pool to cool down and figure out who I was going to stalk next.

When I got there a woman was sitting on one of the deck chairs. She had her head in her hands. Obviously weeping. I stood there for a moment considering what to do. People in that condition usually want to be left alone. I didn't want to embarrass her. But just before I turned she lifted her head and saw me, and went, "Oh!"

Her eyes were red. She was around thirty. Curly blonde hair.

"Didn't mean to startle you," I said.

She shook her head and waved her arm.

"Is there something I can get you?" I said.

"No."

"How about some water?" I said.

"Doesn't matter," she said.

"Is there somebody I can contact for you?"

Her face was a confusion between friendliness and caution.

"I don't mean to intrude," I said. "I just wondered."

"I just..." She took a deep breath. "My dad died."

And the tears flowed again.

I sat in a chair. "I'm sorry. I know what that's like. I lost my dad, too."

"It wasn't a shock," she said. "He had cancer. But it wasn't supposed to be for months. And I wasn't there."

"We can't always control that," I said.

"He told me to come out here," she said. "He told me to go for my dream."

"And what is that?"

"I'm an actor," she said.

I felt even more sorry for her.

"How long have you been here?" I said.

"Three days," she said.

"Anybody with you?"

Her face changed then, in an understandable way.

"Sorry," I said. "That's intrusive and you don't know me. I'll leave you now."

"Wait," she said. "I'm not afraid or anything, sitting out here. Thank you for saying something. You said you lost your dad?"

"Yes."

"How did you deal with it?"

By withdrawing into myself. By remaking my body. By finding the man responsible and killing him. By changing my name. By running from ghosts. By keeping my distance from people. Sometimes by erupting and—

"A day at a time," I said.

"You were close to your father?"

"Very. My mother, too."

"Is she alive?"

"No."

"I'm sorry," she said.

"It's a good and human thing to be sorry," I said. "When a just man dies, sorrow and joy are one."

She blinked a couple of times.

"A poet named Auden wrote that," I said.

"Can I say something?"

"Of course."

"You don't look like somebody who recites poetry."

"I've been told as much."

"Are you a writer or something?"

"I work for a lawyer," I said.

She paused, looking at the pool as if the water held comforting secrets.

"Does it get any easier?" she asked.

"It gets endurable," I said.

"I hope so."

"Do you have someone to help you with funeral, estate, those things?"

"My mom and sister," she said. "I'll be going back on Wednesday."

I gave her one of Ira's cards. "This is the lawyer I work for. He knows good lawyers all over. If you need help finding someone, give him a call. He'll hook you up."

"Thank you," she said.

"If you need anything else, I'm in 24."

"This is amazing."

"Amazing?"

"That you should have come along right at this moment." She pocketed the card. "May I know your name?"

"Mike."

"I'm Jenna."

I heard myself say, "God bless you, Jenna."

"You, too, Mike."

I drove over to the Topanga station of the LAPD. I went to the front desk and told the officer I had some illegal drugs to drop off for disposal. I gave him the baggie of dust.

His look told me this is not something that happens every day. He asked me how I got it and I said I took it away from an acquaintance, which was true enough. He asked me if I'd like to leave my contact information, and I told him they had enough on their hands these days.

And heard myself say, "God bless you guys."

That night I slept better than I had in weeks.

A preliminary hearing in California is a special proceeding held before a judge or magistrate. When the D.A. has filed a criminal complaint, it's their burden to show there's enough evidence to hold the defendant to answer, meaning go to trial. The prosecutor presents witnesses and evidence, subject to cross-examination by the defense.

This prelim was being held in the courtroom of Judge Latoya Frye. Naturally it was all Plexiglas and mask wearing. I had one on, and my best Tommy Bahama Hawaiian shirt, a fashion choice Hope Wynn, the Deputy D.A., apparently did not approve of. She looked at me as if I'd smuggled a ukulele into court and was about to play "Tiny Bubbles." She motioned me to a chair in the gallery and started going through some files at her counsel table.

At the table was the defense lawyer. He looked fresh out of law school but was completely bald, the shaved-head variety. His eyes were close-set, his mouth tight, and his suit off the wrong size rack. He had the look of a Deputy Public Defender.

The public was not allowed in so the courtroom was relatively empty. Detective Coltrane Smith sat on the other side of the gallery. He gave me a nod when we made eye contact.

The door next to the empty jury box opened. A

deputy sheriff came in with Sammie Sand, who was wearing jailhouse blues and handcuffs. The deputy seated Sand at the defense table and removed the cuffs. His lawyer leaned over and said something to him. Sand shook his head.

The bailiff told us all to stand as he announced the judge. Judge Frye looked around forty. Young to be a judge. But that was probably a good thing. She hadn't had time to morph into one of those tired, cynical judges who just take up space on the bench. There was an energetic intelligence in her eyes, meaning there was a possibility to get that rarest of things—actual justice.

She called the case and the two lawyers announced their appearances.

"Hope Wynn for the People," Hope Wynn said.

The other lawyer said, "Seth Pound for the defendant, Mr. Sand."

Hope Wynn called Detective Coltrane Smith to the stand.

He gave a summary of the police report, and the arrest and questioning of the defendant. He said that Sammie Sand did not waive his Miranda rights and insisted on having a lawyer appointed.

Wynn then showed Smith the knife that Sand had wielded at the bookstore. He identified it, and Wynn had it marked as an exhibit.

Seth Pound took a few shots at Detective Smith.

"When you got to the scene, where was Mr. Sand?"

"He was in the police vehicle," Smith said.

"Was he in handcuffs?"

"Yes."

"And he was in handcuffs because the chief witness against him had brutally attacked him."

"Objection," Hope Wynn said.

"Sustained," said Judge Frye. "You want to rephrase that, Mr. Pound?"

"Detective Smith," said Seth Pound, "was it reported to you that Michael Romeo, the prosecution's chief witness, caused Mr. Sand's head to make contact with the ground, on at least three occasions?"

Even with his mask on, I could tell Smith was fighting hard not to smile. "That is correct."

Pound strutted for a moment behind the podium, as if he were thinking of his next earth-shattering question.

"Where was the knife when you first saw it?"

"It was on the bookstore counter."

"Do you know how it got there?"

"I believe Mr. Romeo put it there."

"Ah, Mr. Romeo again."

Hope Wynn stood. "Is there a question, or is this a speech?"

Judge Frye was having none of it. "Mr. Pound, you know better than that. You're not on TV."

"I'm just laying a foundation," Pound said.

"Then do it the right way," Judge Frye said.

"Detective Smith, you never saw the knife in the possession of Mr. Sand, did you?"

"I did not."

"You only saw it after it had been handled by Mr. Romeo, is that correct?"

"That's right."

"For all you know, that knife could belong to Mr. Romeo, couldn't it?"

There was a moment there when everybody seemed stunned. Like they'd heard a distant explosion, not close enough to dive under a table, but enough to command attention.

. . .

That's when I was called. The clerk swore me in and said, "Please state your name and spell your last name for the record, please."

"Mike Romeo. R-O-M-E-O."

Hope Wynn began her questioning. "Mr. Romeo, how are you employed?"

"I work as an investigator for a lawyer, Ira Rosen."

"And were you working in that capacity on the morning of March 1?"

"No."

"Tell the court what you were doing at around ten o'clock that morning."

"I was at a bookstore, the Odyssey, downtown. Browsing and reading."

"And just before the knife attack, what—"

"Objection," defense lawyer Seth Pound said. "Assumes a fact not in evidence."

"Sustained," said the judge. "Re-characterize, Ms. Wynn."

Hope Wynn said, "Just before the incident which is the subject of this hearing, Mr. Romeo, where were you situated?"

"I was outside the front door, sitting in a chair, perusing a copy of Harold Bloom's *Shakespeare: The Invention of the Human.*"

"During your reading, did something happen that caused you to look up from your book?"

"Yes."

"Please tell us what that was."

"It was the defendant walking into the store with criminal intent."

"Objection," Seth Pound said. "The witness is offering an opinion."

Hope Wynn said, "I'll lay the foundation."

"Then I'll overrule the objection," Judge Frye said. "But let's get some facts."

"Thank you, Your Honor," the prosecutor said. "Was there something you saw that caused you to form the opinion that the defendant had what you call criminal intent?"

"Yes."

"And what was that?"

"He had a knife."

"Can you describe the knife?"

"It was a knife with about a six-inch blade."

Hope Wynn stepped from the podium to her counsel table and picked something up. "Your Honor, I have what has been previously marked as People's Exhibit One. May I approach the witness?"

"You may," said the judge.

Hope Wynn came up to the witness box and showed me the exhibit.

"Mr. Romeo, is this the knife that you saw in the defendant's hand?"

"Objection."

"Sustained."

"Mr. Romeo, does this look like the knife you saw in the defendant's hand?"

"Yes."

"Is there anything else that caused you to form the opinion of criminal intent?"

"It was the way he was holding the knife," I said. "Up against his forearm, so it was hidden."

"Can you show the court?"

"Objection," Seth Pound said.

"Overruled," the judge said.

Hope Wynn handed me the knife. I stood so the judge

could see my arm. I showed her the knife position I'd observed.

Judge Frye said, "The record will reflect that the witness is holding the knife in his left hand, with the blade against his forearm, facing up toward the elbow."

"Thank you, Your Honor." Hope Wynn took the knife from me and put it back on the counsel table.

Back at the podium she said, "What did you do next, Mr. Romeo?"

"I got up and went into the store. I saw him—the defendant—walking quickly toward the front counter. There was an employee there, named Wanda."

"Did you know Wanda?"

"From the bookstore, yes. Back when it was open before the lockdown."

"What did you do next?"

"I prevented the defendant from killing Wanda."

"Objection!" Seth Pound said.

"Sustained," said the judge. "Mr. Romeo, just tell the court what action you took."

"I threw the book at him, Your Honor."

"You did what?"

"Well, it was the Harold Bloom book. I threw it at his head. It did the trick."

"Let me understand," the judge said. "You threw a book at Mr. Sand's head?"

"It's a thick book," I said. "Perfect for a thick head."

No one laughed. Hope Wynn winced. Sammie Sand gave me the hard-eye of the prison yard.

"This isn't a comedy, Mr. Romeo," Judge Frye said.

"I apologize, Your Honor," I said.

"Go ahead, Ms. Wynn."

"What effect did your book have on the defendant?" Hope Wynn said.

"It dropped him," I said.

"And what did you do next?"

"I put a knee on his back and removed the knife from his hand."

"How did you do that?"

"By slamming his wrist on the ground. Then I held him down until the police arrived."

Hope Wynn picked up her yellow pad and flipped to a new page. "Now, Mr. Romeo, while you had the defendant on the ground, did you do something to his head?"

"Yes," I said.

"Tell the court what you did."

I looked at the judge. "Your Honor, he was cursing a blue streak, as my grandfather used to put it. So I tweaked him with my middle finger and told him to be quiet."

Hope Wynn said, "Did he cease cursing?"

"No," I said. "He screamed something else."

"What did he scream?"

"You want his exact words?"

"Yes."

I gave them. And considered it a subtle victory that the judge's eyebrows went up.

Hope Wynn said, "What did you do in response to those words?"

"I grabbed his hair and tapped the floor with his head."

"Tapped?" said the judge.

"It may have been a little more than a tap, Your Honor. I just wanted to get his attention and stop the cursing."

Judge Frye frowned, and nodded at Hope Wynn to continue.

"Did he stop cursing?"

"No."

"What, if anything, did you do then?"

"I gave the floor another tap with his head, harder this

time. That's when he stopped talking."

"Did you knock him out?"

"I dazed him. He got the message."

"Mr. Romeo, do you have any previous association with the defendant?"

"No."

"Do you have any personal animosity toward the defendant?"

"Only the general animosity I have toward social miscreants."

The stenographer said, "I'm sorry, what was that last word?"

"Miscreants," I said.

"Would you mind spelling that?"

"M-I-S-C-R-E-A-N-T-S."

Honestly, I thought it the right word for the sentiment.

But Hope Wynn was not amused. She wanted this thing wrapped up. "So your answer is that you do not have any personal—"

"Objection," said Seth Pound. "Leading."

"I'll allow it," Judge Frye said, "as I think it may be Ms. Wynn's last question."

"That's entirely correct, Your Honor," Hope Wynn said.

"Nothing personal against the defendant," I said.

Hope Wynn sat down.

Seth Pound stood up.

H e buttoned his coat like a suit of armor, ready for battle.

He stepped to the podium with his legal pad and said, "Michael Romeo. Is that your real name?"

"Yes," I said.

"I mean, is that the name you were born with?"

"Objection," I said.

Pound looked at me like I'd licked his microphone.

The judge seemed equally stunned. "Mr. Romeo, you can't object."

"Why not, Your Honor?" I said.

"Because that's the lawyer's job."

I glanced at Hope Wynn. She shook her head.

Call me Mr. Persistent. "I don't know if that's the law, Your Honor."

"In my courtroom it is," Judge Frye said.

"I've read the Evidence Code," I said. "And Mr. Pound's question is irrelevant to any material fact."

The momentary silence in the courtroom I counted as a minor victory. Judge Frye tapped the eraser end of a pencil on her desk.

Finally, the judge said, "Mr. Pound, what is the relevance of your question?"

Seth Pound said, "The credibility of the witness, Your Honor. If he is hiding something, we have a right to know it."

"Not without an offer of proof," I said.

Judge Frye said, "Did you go to law school, Mr. Romeo?"

"I just read a lot."

"That can get you into trouble. However, in this instance you are correct. Mr. Pound, what is your offer of proof?"

"Your Honor, the witness has asserted that his name is Michael Romeo. We have evidence that this is not his birth name. We also have evidence of his recent past, which presents troubling incidents of random violence. Under Ms. Wynn's questioning, the witness has admitted to pummeling my client's head into the floor, for no other reason than his malformed opinion that he didn't like the way my client looked. Whatever that word was he used—"

"Miscreant," I said.

"Quiet, Mr. Romeo," Judge Frye said. "Not another word out of you. Please continue, Mr. Pound."

"This calls into question his credibility as a witness," Seth Pound said. "This is crucial, as he is the only one offering testimony concerning an alleged attack."

Judge Frye paused a moment, then said, "You may proceed, Mr. Pound. And Mr. Romeo, no more objections from you. That's up to Ms. Wynn."

I wanted to object to that, but decided to keep my mouth shut. For once.

Preening like a pink flamingo, Seth Pound said, "What was your birth name?"

"Michael Chamberlain," I said.

"And you were born where?"

"New Haven, Connecticut."

"Subsequently, you changed your name, from Chamberlain to Romeo, correct?"

"Yes."

"Why did you change your name?"

There is the truth, and then there is the whole truth. One of my rules is you don't owe the truth to those who lie. A corollary is you don't owe the whole truth to those who will weaponize it to pervert justice. I was not going to tell Seth Pound or anyone else that I changed my name after hunting down the man responsible for the murder of my parents. Instead, I gave him the short version.

"I began to do some professional fighting," I said. "I thought the name Romeo sounded better. Also, I'm a Shakespeare fan."

"I'm sure we're all happy to know that."

"Objection," Hope Wynn said.

"Sustained," Judge Frye said. "You know better than that, Mr. Pound."

"You have used your false name to deceive people, isn't that true?" said Pound.

"It's not a false name," I said.

"Do you have proof of a legal name change?"

I had an illicit driver's license. I did not whip it out to show him.

"No," I said.

Hope Wynn again objected and this time Judge Frye told the defense lawyer she'd heard enough.

Pound said, "You testified you saw my client holding a knife against his forearm, correct?"

"Yes."

"He never changed the position of the knife, did he?"

"No, but—"

"You've answered the question."

"But I want to say—"

Judge Frye said, "Just answer the question you are asked, Mr. Romeo. Ms. Wynn can follow up if she needs to."

"She'll need to," I said.

Seth Pound turned a page on his legal pad. "You said on direct that you told my client to be quiet. In fact, you actually told him to *shut up*, isn't that true?"

"I don't really remember."

"Do you remember giving a statement to the police?"

"Yes."

"And in that statement, didn't you say you used the words 'shut up'?"

"I may have."

"And how many times was it that you slammed my client's head into the floor?"

"I wouldn't say slammed."

"What word would you use, Mr. Romeo?"

"Knocked?"

"It was enough to render my client unconscious, was it

not?"

"Dazed was the word I used."

"Isn't it true that you shot and killed a Nevada sheriff last year?"

The little Nimrod had done his homework. And he was using the cross-examiner's trick of quickly switching subjects to throw me off guard.

I stayed on guard and said, "A corrupt sheriff and it was self-defense and I can connect you with the FBI agent who can so attest."

"Isn't this a pattern with you, Mr. Romeo? A pattern of mayhem and death?"

"Enough of this, Your Honor," Hope Wynn said.

"I agree," said Judge Frye.

"Mr. Romeo," Pound said, his voice dripping with TV-drama revulsion, "you never saw my client holding a knife in an attacking manner, did you?"

"He was about to," I said.

"Are you psychic?"

"Objection," Hope Wynn said.

"Sustained," Judge Frye said.

Seth Pound didn't miss a beat. "In point of fact you never saw my client holding a knife at all, did you?"

That got some steam coming out my ears. "Of course I saw it. And everybody saw it after he hit the floor."

"After he hit the floor," Seth Pound said. "No more questions."

The judge called for a fifteen-minute recess. Hope Wynn had no desire to talk to me. She disappeared from the courtroom through a side door. A deputy sheriff took Sammie Sand back to the lockup. Seth Pound went out to the hallway, holding a phone to his ear.

I was free to go but wanted to see how this thing was going to wrap up. Almost always a judge binds a defendant over for trial. This seemed—at least to me—like a slam dunk. There were enough facts to get this bozo in front of a jury. Oh, joyous day. I'd get to testify again.

I took a seat in the front row of the gallery and lowered my mask under my chin. The bailiff gave me a look, but in an act of human decency said nothing.

Detective Coltrane Smith sat down next to me. He had his mask on, owing to his professional responsibility.

"You're sticking around?" he said.

"Just curious," I said. "How'd I do on the stand?"

"I loved it, but I don't think the judge did."

"I know the prosector wasn't too pleased."

"They're hard to please as it is," he said. "Especially now."

"Now?"

"New D.A. Not exactly a law-and-order type. You get into the D.A.'s office to put bad guys away. When you get orders from up top not to prosecute certain offenders, or go for certain enhancements, it doesn't sit well. Same goes for cops. Getting harder and harder to do our jobs. It's why L.A. is hemorrhaging officers."

"It's the same in most major cities," I said.

"So let me ask you a question."

"Sure."

"You're a private investigator, right?"

I shook my head. "I investigate for a lawyer. You don't need a license for that."

"Ah," he said. "Cause I was thinking of getting my own ticket. Just wondering about the lay of the land."

"With your background I don't think you'd have any trouble getting work. A good anchor client or two, like a big insurance company, and you'd be set."

"Awfully tempting, the way things are now."

"If you ever make the move, give me a call." I gave him an Ira card.

"You're all right," Detective Coltrane Smith said. He put out his hand. I shook it heartily. Some things are worth preserving, and the handshake is one of them.

The bailiff announced that court was again in session.

Judge Frye said, "After considering the evidence, the witness statements, and making my own assessment of the veracity of same, my ruling is that there is no probable cause to bind Mr. Sand over for trial. Accordingly, the People's information is dismissed and the bond is discharged. The bailiff will see to Mr. Sand's release."

Boom.

Just like that.

Sammie Sand gave Seth Pound a fist bump, then shot me a glare.

Hope Wynn gave me a similar look.

A little dazed and definitely ticked off, I emerged from the criminal courthouse onto Temple Street and found Sammie Sand waiting for me.

With a bigger and older version of himself.

His ex-con father, no doubt. His massive arms were tatted up and folded across his chest. He was shaved up top but had a thick, gray Fu Manchu mustache.

I gave them a quick glance, then walked away.

"Yo!" Daddy Sand said.

I ignored him.

"Hey!" Sammie said.

I kept strolling along, turning left at Hill Street.

A puffing Sammie Sand ran past me, stopped. "We wanna talk to you."

Daddy Sand came next, walking fast.

"No time, boys," I said. "I've got to catch *Judge Judy*."

"Chill," Daddy said. His voice was like a bucket of rocks. "What's your game? How come you're after your own?"

"My own?"

"What's your color?"

"Magenta," I said. "Look out."

"Listen," Daddy said. "We got to stick together. They're coming for us. Don't you know that?"

"I've got no use for you or your spawn," I said.

"You're gonna regret it."

"I regret this whole day," I said, then gave Daddy a prison stare. "Which one of your sons is the sniper?"

He frowned.

"Which one shot the cop?" I said.

There was no tell in his expression. "What are you talkin' about?"

"Because I'll find out," I said.

"Find out *what*?"

"That's enough for today." I started to move around Daddy, but he stepped in front of me. "You be careful now."

"Oh, so we're starting with the prison threats?" I said. "Striking fear into my little heart?"

Sammie spat a curse at me, bringing my mother into it.

To Daddy I said, "If I ever so much as see his shadow, I'll cut out his tongue and use it to clean my pans. That goes for the rest of the fruit of your loins. And you, too."

We locked eyes like a couple of lifers, waiting for the other to make the next move. Finally, Daddy wagged his finger at me, smiled, turned, and told Sammie to come on. They walked back up to Temple and disappeared.

. . .

I walked half a block to the park area between City Hall and the Music Center. I sat on a bench and watched the people for awhile. Downtown was getting a bit more lively again, people walking around. Of course, they had to avoiding the homeless sleeping on cardboard and the shirtless schizophrenic screaming on the corner.

At least no throats were being cut at the moment. We should be grateful for the little things.

An old man in a wheelchair was being pushed by a nurse-looking lady. Both were masked up. His eyes were fixed and dull, any interest in life long since dead inside him. Riding out his days.

Directly behind him, a shaggy-haired guy in his twenties skateboarded by. It was like the old man's lost youth giving a final wave before the groundhog started delivering his mail.

Two women, dressed like professionals, walking with purpose, talking with animation, came my way. I wouldn't have paid them more than passing attention, except the one not wearing a mask looked familiar.

She glanced my way, and smiled her recognition.

She said something to her companion that might have been *See you later.* The companion nodded and walked on.

Then Agent Holly Samara of the DEA came over to me and said, "Well, look who's here."

O ur paths had crossed before over a Mexican cartel and designer drug case. I'd be lying to you if I said it wasn't a pleasant path. Holly Samara looks like one of those agents that is played by an attractive actress on TV. You know, the kind that doesn't exist in real life. Except in this case.

She sat on the bench. Her chestnut hair was cut short.

It gave her an elfin look that was counterbalanced by intelligent brown eyes.

"What brings you downtown?" she said.

"I testified," I said.

"In a trial?"

"A preliminary hearing."

"Do tell."

I gave her the short version. I left out the after meeting with Daddy and Son.

"And what about you?" I said.

"I had a meeting at the Federal courthouse," she said. "I'll be testifying, too."

She looked at her watch. "Let's get a drink."

It was the perfect invitation for a time such as this. We went to a place Holly knew on 2nd Street.

We sat at a table in the bar area. It was an L.A. kind of place with windows letting in plenty of sunlight.

I said, "You favor Grey Goose martinis, if I recall."

"How sweet of you to remember," she said.

"I'm sweet for two minutes a day," I said.

"So I caught you at the right time," she said.

"The two minutes is almost up."

"Maybe we can do something about that."

She looked at me directly, and it was one heck of a look. As confident as if she had two hands on her Glock and was telling me to put my hands on the wall.

The gaze was broken by a young server. I ordered the Grey Goose martini for Agent Samara, and a Corona for me.

When the server left, Agent Samara said, "I like that you ordered the drinks."

"You do?"

"It doesn't happen anymore," she said. "All the men in this town are too afraid. There's been a mass emasculation."

I cleared my throat.

"I think you're an exception," she said.

"You have a direct approach," I said.

"I don't like wasting time," she said.

"I'm glad I ran into you," I said.

She smiled. "Keep going."

"Because I'm working a drug angle."

Her smile faded. "Oh."

"Vector Dust," I said. "I have a client, a high school kid, caught dealing. I wonder if there's a cartel involved somewhere."

She shook her head. "Not since the deal."

"What deal?"

"Between organized crime here and the cartels in Mexico. The cartels import drugs through a porous border. It's no accident that there's a so-called crisis down there. It's all part of the deal."

"The government's involved?"

She gave me a practiced shrug, one that said *I can say no more.*

But she did say, "The Border Patrol is overwhelmed with the migrants, the women and children. It's beyond their scope. That leaves other parts of the border open for importation of opioids. And then organized crime takes over through franchises."

"Franchises?"

"Just like a McDonald's. There are heads of local franchises who pay tribute to the crime families, and get to operate. That's what you're looking at."

"So a kid who is selling at a local high school is like a burger flipper. But he has a manager. And the manager has a franchise owner."

She took a breath in a way that told me she didn't like the topic.

"Maybe we shouldn't discuss business," I said.

"That's a good idea," she said. "I'm full up with it. I almost said I'm fed up with it."

"A fed-up fed," I said.

"So many things wrong, under the surface, above the surface, from the brass and from—Hey, we said no business."

"How about those Dodgers?" I said.

"Mike, how have you been? What have you been doing?"

"Still working for Ira Rosen. Living in Paradise Cove."

"Nice."

"It can be, as long as people who want to hurt you don't find you there."

Her eyebrows went up. They came down as our server placed our drinks in front of us.

I clinked my Corona bottle on her martini glass and we drank.

"I'll tell you something, Mike,"Agent Samara said. "I think about you a lot."

"That's got to be a real pain," I said. "Like sciatica."

"I know you're a loose cannon. And I'm sworn to uphold the law. That makes for an awkward relationship."

"Are we in a relationship?"

"Like a soldier and a nurse who once met in a field hospital. Now, here we are again."

"You're going to make me blush, Agent Samara."

"If you call me that again I'll toss this drink in your face."

"I believe you," I said. "Holly."

"You know, last time we talked you were a little ambiguous about being involved with someone. You can tell me if you are, and that'll be the end of the personal side of things."

"I'm all about ambiguity," I said. "Or maybe something else."

"What's her name?" Holly said.

"There's no getting around you, is there?"

"I'm good at my job."

"Sophie."

"You say that with a tone of resignation," Holly said.

"A good word," I said.

"I've been resigned, too," she said. "Like you, I know that what I do is not exactly conducive to romantic attachments. You don't think about that cost when you're young. You just see the opportunity and walk through the door. At some point the door slams and locks and you look around and wonder what happened."

"You can always quit," I said.

"And do what?"

"Something different."

"Oh, thank you very much."

She sipped her drink.

"Or I can find someone who is just as vulnerable as I am," she said. "What are you doing the rest of your life?"

It was a good question, one that cut me between the ribs.

I said, "I think I need some time to mull this over."

"Just what I was thinking," she said. "Let's continue this conversation at my place. I'll make you my famous pasta carbonara with pan-seared scallops."

"Famous the world over?"

"At least from here to Downey."

"I'm being hunted by a killer right now," I said.

"You'll never be safer than with me and my pasta and my Glock, and a nice bottle of wine."

"You make a good point."

"I always do," she said.

Holly Samara lived in a apartment building off Wilshire, over near UCLA. It was a tidy one bedroom, decked out in earthy colors—ochre, greens, deep reds, soft blues. A place for a busy DEA agent to come back to and relax. There was even a pot by the window with—

"Begonias," I said.

"You know about flowers?"

"It's a hobby of mine."

Holly looked at me with a bemused smile. "You are full of surprises. Can I offer you a glass of wine?"

"Yes," I said. "Something frolicsome but not rebellious, with a whisper of oak and counterintelligence."

"I have just the thing," she said.

"Mind if I make a phone call?"

"Step out on the balcony if you like."

I did. And called Ira.

"The prelim did not go well," I said.

"Do you want to tell me why?"

"Not now. I'm dining with an old acquaintance."

"Care to tell me who?"

"Holly Samara, the DEA agent, remember? I bumped into her downtown, right after the Sand family threatened me. So I'll be here a bit and—"

"Hold it! What's this about the Sand family?"

"Oh yeah. Sammie Sand and his dear old dad were waiting for me outside the courthouse. Gave me a little business. I gave a little right back. You know how it goes."

"For you, yes, I know how it goes."

"I accused them of being behind the snipe. Didn't seem

to be any reaction. Still, I wouldn't rule them out. Stay left of bang."

"Always do," Ira said.

B ack inside, a glass of white wine was waiting for me on the dining room table. I sat and watched Holly prepping the food. She'd put on some jazz.

"Diana Krall?" I said.

"Very good," she said. "Is there anything you don't know?"

"I'm a little shaky on the eighteenth century Ottoman Empire," I said. "But other than that..."

"We'll have to brush up," she said.

From there we dropped into easy conversation, which I guided toward her side of the ledger. We talked about her grandfather, who'd been an L.A. cop in the days of Chief William Parker. He'd retired under his favorite chief, Daryl Gates, in 1986.

When she started probing for more of my story, I mostly deflected.

"You really are a mystery man, aren't you?" she said.

"International," I said.

"You know, I don't cook for just anybody. You're going to have to give a little."

"Maybe in time," I said.

"Time is what we have," she said. "I've got the rest of the week off."

I sipped my wine.

S he was right about the meal. Exquisite. We ate and spoke of things other than business. I found out she loved the Dodgers and Union Station. A real Angeleno she was. And thus just as despondent about the state of the city as most locals these days.

When we were finished we sat in her living room with coffee and listened to more jazz, classic and contemporary —Ella Fitzgerald, Stacey Kent, Nina Simone. When Cassandra Wilson came on with her seductive "Don't Explain," Holly told me that could be our theme song.

"Ours?" I said.

She leaned toward me, put her hand behind my head, and kissed me.

"Stay with me tonight," she whispered.

It took me a moment to catch my breath. And another to figure out what to say.

"Ninety percent..." I said.

"Of what?" she said.

"Of my body, screaming at me to say yes."

She pulled me in and kissed me again, hard.

Coming up for air, I said, "Make that ninety-five percent."

"Then it's settled."

I said nothing.

"Isn't it?" she said.

"Holly, I've messed up a lot of my life because of the ninety-five percent. I've used women, I've killed men... wait, you're law enforcement."

"Not tonight," she said.

"The five percent is what keeps us from becoming animals," I said.

Holly sat up, straight and stiff, her eyes aflame. "That's what you think this is?"

"Bad choice of words," I said.

"You got that right." She stood, walked over to the window, her back to me.

I got up and went to her. "Would it help if I changed the word from animal to brute?"

With considerable consternation she said, "What are you talking about?"

"Can I try to explain? Just once?"

With a deep sigh, she turned around. "Once."

"Maybe I do think too much," I said. "But I don't know any other way. I lean philosophical. Maybe it's a curse, maybe it isn't. All I know is, it's me."

"Philosophical..."

"Here it is, Holly. There's a stark raving difference between Eros and the brute. The object of Eros is a person. The object of the brute is his own satisfaction. The brute wants only pleasure from a woman. Eros wants to be completed by *the* woman. One night years ago I woke up with someone beside me, weeping, and knew I was a brute. I didn't want to be that anymore."

She pondered a moment.

She said, "So what is your philosophical conclusion about the two of us, Socrates?"

"I don't have a conclusion," I said. "Yet."

"Hurry it up," she said. "I'm not going to wait around."

"Understood," I said.

"And one other thing."

"Yes?"

"I hate philosophy."

The hardest thing to figure out, the ancient sages knew, is your own messed-up self (translated loosely from the Greek). This is especially true in matters of amour. D.H. Lawrence may have had it right in his poem, that we've made a great mess of love.

Othello smothers Desdemona, then pitifully declares

that he loved not wisely, but too well. To Cleopatra, Antony says, "We have kissed away kingdoms and provinces."

The romantic poets were adamant that there is no greater happiness than that which is found in love. But they had to admit there is no greater misery, no despair more searing, than love lost or unrequited.

Did I even want to mess with the mess of love?

Mike Romeo, boy philosopher, trying to solve the mysteries of the heart going 80 mph on the 405. And the last thing I wanted to do was spy on a real estate agent with a penchant for serial affairs.

I searched Mandi McGuane's website and found the four active homes she repped. Two in Porter Ranch, one in Northridge, and one in Chatsworth. It would take a lot of driving to cover them all, but I remembered Joey Feint finding some damning information just by looking at a house. His client was a middle-aged woman who suspected her husband of having an affair with a "floozy." Joey found the floozy's house and scoped it, noticing a pair of deck shoes in the corner of the porch. The shoes were too big for a woman, and were well worn. They also had faded script that read *Shennecossett Yacht Club.* Soon enough Joey had photos of the illicit couple *in flagrante delicto* aboard a, ahem, pleasure craft.

I started with the Porter Ranch properties. Both had Mandi's sign with that overconfident picture of her. One of the houses looked occupied, so I gave it just a cursory glance. The other Porter Ranch house didn't have any activity going on and no cars were in the driveway. I watched it for five minutes.

From there it was a short drop down into Northridge. The Mandi McGuane property there had, as they say in the biz, curb appeal. It also had two little kids playing in the front yard with what could have been the dad. But you never know these days.

I stopped and got out.

The man looked at me warily.

"Saw the sign," I said. "I'm looking to buy."

"Oh," he said. "Sure."

"Can I have a look?"

"There's an open house this weekend. Let me give you a flyer."

"Great."

He went into the house, taking the kids—a boy and a girl—with him. I wouldn't have left them out there with me, either.

The man came back and handed me a color flyer with all the info, and that Mandi smile.

"Mandi McGuane," I said. "She's hard to miss."

"Yeah," the man said. "Persistent. And she's very, very good."

"Know her well?"

"I've gotten to," he said.

"Does she work with anyone? A partner maybe?"

He shook his head. "Not that I know of."

"Okay," I said. "My name's Phil. Maybe I'll see you this weekend."

"I'm David. Hope so."

Chatsworth is nestled in the northwest part of the Valley. It was an early success owing to the railroad coming through in 1893. That gave the farmers access to a much larger market for their crops. When they decided to bore a tunnel through the Santa Susana mountains, workers from all over the country came in for the job, which was completed in 1904. The town became known for its oranges, lemons, and grapes. Also, for thoroughbred horse ranches.

Lucy and Desi had a big spread out here, adding to the glamour.

Like all other parts of the Valley, there were boom times and lean times, leaving good parts and not-so-good parts.

Of course, Mandi McGuane only bought and sold in the good parts.

I pulled up at the address. And right there in front of the house was Mandi's BMW.

Right behind it was a pickup truck. One familiar to me.

Serendipity!

And a suspicion of what was happening inside.

The Romeo school of lock-picking was again in session. I popped the door open a crack and listened. Voices—and a giggle—came from a distant part of the house. I padded into the nicely appointed living room and had a seat. There was a copy of *Better Homes & Gardens* on a side table. I picked it up, opened it, and cleared my throat.

The voices stopped. And thankfully the giggling, too.

A moment later Mandi McGuane came into the room, her hair a bit disheveled.

She stopped on a proverbial dime when she recognized me. There was an immediate transformation of the facial features, from confused hostess to enraged Medusa. If she could have turned me to stone, she would have.

"What... what..." she hissed.

Before she could find the words, Brian Cunningham came in, tucking his shirt in his jeans.

"Have I interrupted something?" I said.

If Mandi was Medusa, Brian was Zeus... and I was Prometheus, about to be chained to a rock so an eagle could eat my liver.

His fists were balled and his face a dangerous shade of red.

"Don't go off half—" I quickly changed my phrasing. "—mad."

"Get out of here!" Mandi said. "I'm calling the police."

"Please do," I said. "We can all discuss matters like civilized folks. I'll bring your brokerage into it, too. They'll be interested in how you, um, show properties."

Brian Cunningham, "What are you doing here?"

I tossed the magazine on the table. "I'll be doing the asking. Why don't you lovebirds have a seat?"

"This is outrageous!" Mandi said.

"Unorthodox, I'll grant you," I said. "But you're a negotiator. You know when you're out-leveraged. And that's what you are. Now sit down."

The unhappy couple exchanged a look. Then they went to the sofa and made themselves, as it were, at home.

"I'm curious," I said. "What is Clint Cunningham's father doing here with the mother of one of Clint's classmates?"

"Why is that your business?" Mandi said.

"My business is to find out what people aren't telling me," I said.

"What's the big deal?" Brian said. "We're seeing each other. We know each other from Elias. You got a problem with that?"

"I never clog the highway of love," I said. "I'm only interested in matters criminal."

"We aren't doing anything illegal," Mandi said.

"Between the two of you, no," I said. "But let's cast a wider net. You both have sons in trouble."

Mandi shot to her feet. "What's happened to Gavin?"

I said, "The trouble I'm talking about is somewhat nefarious. I told Gavin I had no intention of telling you about it, and that was true at the time. But intentions change with the circumstances."

"So what is it?" Mandi said.

"Gavin has been selling test information to students, with the help of another classmate, one Bianca Aiken."

This news sent Mandi back to a sitting position as she issued a one-syllable curse.

"I warned him!" she said.

"Might not get into Harvard," I said.

This pushed her over whatever edge she'd been teetering on. She started screaming. Her words were aflame with Fs and Ss, and in between a ramble on how she was doing everything she could to make sure her only child got every advantage in life, but people keep coming around to eff things up, and that included me... and Brian.

"Me?" Brian said. "What do I have to do with this?"

Mandi said, "You and your lousy kid!"

Brian asked her what the eff Clint ever did to Gavin, and then the two of them effed back and forth at each other in a discordant symphony of blame and recrimination.

I sat there like some ignored relationship counselor letting his clients hash it out.

Finally, I said, "Children! Enough! I'm going to find out what I want to know if it takes all night."

They stopped their match and looked at me for the next move.

Which Mandi made. "Gavin was never in trouble until he took up with Clint Cunningham."

"Oh, come on!" Brian said.

"One at a time," I said.

"It's true!" Mandi said. "A four-point-five GPA, soccer team, student council. But after Clint came along he started to slide."

Brian Cunningham looked like he wanted to say something, but was being prevented by some sort of force field emanating out of Mandi McGuane. He put his head back on the sofa.

"Right?" Mandi said. "Am I right?"

"I don't know," Brian said.

"Because you don't want to know," Mandi said.

"Let's see if we can work this out," I said. "Because I'd hate to be the one to bring trouble to this budding romance. If each of you gives a little, maybe we can all go home happy."

"I just wish you'd go away," Mandi said.

"I intend to, believe me. Just so I get the story straight. Your claim is that Clint somehow dragged Gavin down."

Mandi nodded.

I asked Brian. "Do you think what Ms. McGuane here suggests is possible?"

Defeated, Brian said, "I guess."

"Would you guess it could be drug related?"

He threw up his hands. "How would I know? I don't see him."

"You know that Clint is pretty gifted when it comes to drawing."

"Yeah, sure, since he was a kid."

"And poetry," I said.

"Poetry?" Brian said. "I don't know anything about that."

"Let me describe to you a picture Clint drew," I said. "Of a skull, looking like death, with blood dripping from the teeth. He's holding a gun and pointing it at his temple. In the empty eye sockets are two letters, T and B. In the mouth is a letter D, with a snake coming out of it."

"Good God," Mandi McGuane said.

"What's the TBD?" Brian said.

"To Be Done," Mandi said.

"Maybe," I said. "Or a reference to persons, with the D being death."

The two of them noodled on that. Followed by blank stares.

"Your ex-wife's name is Trista," I said. "Your name is Brian."

"Wait, what?" Brian said.

"Might your son be wishing the two of you to be dead?"

That hit him like a punch in the nose.

"And if so, why?" I said.

Brian shook his head. "Man, I didn't see that coming."

"Nothing in Clint's behavior to make you think he'd be holding such thoughts about you?"

"We had fights, the usual stuff. But never anything like this."

"He's sixteen," Mandi said. "Overdramatic."

"You don't know anything about him," Brian said.

"I know enough," Mandi said.

"What does that mean?" Brian said.

"I know he cries when he doesn't get his way."

I jumped in. "How do you know that?"

"I saw it," Mandi said. "He was over at the house awhile ago, with that girl that goes with Gavin now. They were in the backyard talking about something when I got home. I saw them out there. Clint had his head down. The girl was talking. Then Gavin. Then Clint started crying."

"What was the reaction of the other two?" I asked.

"Non-committal."

"Did you talk to them?" I said.

"No, it was better they were left alone. I went upstairs and did some work on the computer. I heard them leave."

"Them?"

"It must have been all three, with Gavin driving."

"Did you ask Gavin what the conversation was about?" I said.

"I mentioned it," Mandi said. "He said it wasn't anything and didn't talk about it further."

"It was obviously about something," I said.

Brian looked at Mandi. "You never told me about that."

"I'm supposed to tell you everything?" she said.

I said, "I've got a feeling both of you aren't telling me things, and that causes me to become annoyed. People generally don't like it when I become annoyed." I stood. "And if I find things out that I should have been told, I move from annoyed to irked. You don't want to see me irked, do you?"

They said nothing, but I think Mandi nodded.

"Here is what I think," I said. "There's drug traffic at Elias, and Clint got caught up in it. But he's not the head of the snake. Whoever that is, Clint's afraid of him, and won't give up a name. TBD may be a clue to the name, or may mean nothing at all concerning this case. But if I were to select someone able to manipulate Clint, I would at this point choose Gavin McGuane. I don't think he is the head of the snake, either, but he may know who it is."

"I do not believe that," Mandi said.

"You should," Brian said.

That brought a fresh, curse-laden rebuke from Mandi McGuane.

"Enough!" I said. "Do either of you know the name Shibuk?"

Brian said, "No."

"I don't think so," Mandi said. "Who is it?"

"That's all for now," I said. "You can go back to your regularly scheduled meeting."

If there's such a thing as a sheepish look, I saw it from both of them.

. . .

I got back to the motel as dusk settled on the city. I missed home, the beach, where I could have watched the orange sun descend into the dark Pacific. I put on jazz and did some push-ups and crunches. Then I jotted some notes in my chrono-log.

As I was finishing up I heard a soft knock at the door. I went to the peephole.

It was Jenna, from the pool.

I opened up.

"Hi," she said. "I saw your light."

"You want to come in?"

"No, I'm getting ready to fly back home. I just wanted to tell you I saw two men at your door earlier today."

"Oh? What did they look like?"

"One of them had a suit on. The other one looked like some kind of biker, I guess."

"Big, tattoos, that sort of thing?"

She shook her head. "He wasn't all that big, but he looked like he was in shape. And he was Asian."

"You would make a good detective," I said.

"Maybe I've watched too many crime shows," she said. "But I took pictures of their car anyway."

She held up her phone.

The car in the picture looked like the one that carried the little man and Nick when they came to see me in Paradise Cove. She swiped, and a pic of the license plate appeared.

"You are brilliant," I said. I took out my phone and took a picture of the license plate.

"So," I said, "you're all set to leave?"

"Yeah. But I'll be back."

"To follow the dream."

"That's what you've got to do," she said.

"Indeed," I said.

She put her hand out. I shook it.

"Stay safe," she said.

"Safe travels," I said.

C onvinced it was San Dae-Ho she had described, I went down to Spinoza. I popped the trunk and got the tire iron and wrapped it in a beach towel. I didn't know if I was being watched or not. But I was hoping Mr. Dae-Ho would return. It was long past time for us to chat.

Back in the room I called Ira.

"I've got a license plate for you to trace," I said.

"Let's have it."

I gave it to him. He told me to do something productive until he called back.

I opened to the last chapter of *The Long Goodbye*. Twist ending. Just what you'd expect from Chandler. And, more and more, what I was expecting from the Clint Cunningham case. Which meant it was time to do some out-of-box thinking.

I went to the room table and opened my log to the first page. Here I recorded in summary all the people I'd questioned. The names were listed in order.

C lint Cunningham
    Trista Cunningham
Bianca Aiken
Brian Cunningham
Nick
Mandi McGuane
Shane McGuane

Gavin McGuane
John _____ (Nick's landlord)
Danny Durant

Next, I removed a blank page from the notebook and set it on the table, lengthwise. In the upper left quadrant I wrote *Mandi McGuane*. In the lower right, *Brian Cunningham*. I drew a line connecting the two.

In the upper right, *Bianca Aiken*. In the lower left, *Gavin McGuane*, and a line connecting them. I now had four names and a big X on the page.

At the bottom of the page I wrote *TBD*. I drew a line from the *T* and wrote *Trista*. And one from the *B* for *Brian*.

It hit me there should be another *B* for *Bianca*. She'd broken up with Clint. Maybe that's why he was crying the way Mandi McGuane had described. Maybe that would be enough for a troubled sixteen-year-old to fantasize about her death.

Ira called back.

"Curious," he said. "The car is registered to a corporation called Verecundus Libri."

"Libri is book," I said. "Verecundus is modesty."

"Very good. What's another word for modest?"

"Humble. Shy. Bashful."

"Work with shy. What do you see?"

"Shy book?" Ding ding ding. "Shibuk, the name."

"Coincidence?"

"Hardly," I said.

"So how is it out there on the street, translated like this?"

"I got that name from Danny Durant," I said. "Could be a code for the corporation. But what does it do? Where is it located?"

"Every California corporation is required to have a physical address and an agent for service of process."

"Which you've got, you clever genius you."

"The name is Adrian Hart. I did a search. He appears to be a CPA."

"Any pictures?"

"None."

He gave me the address, an office building on Ventura Boulevard in Encino.

"I'll see what I can turn up tomorrow," I said.

"That would be the correct deadline," Ira said. "Clint's been granted an emergency hearing on Friday afternoon."

"Three days."

"Two and a half."

"You'll want me to testify."

"I'd rather submit your affidavit."

"Why?"

"I'll issue a subpoena for the deputy who saw Clint's outburst. If he doesn't show, I may be able to get a continuance."

"Gamesmanship," I said.

"The law is not a game, but it is a gamble. You have to know how to improve the odds."

"I'll bet on you anytime, Ira."

"I love you too, Michael."

That night I slept on the floor, under the window, the tire iron by my side. If a midnight visitor were to break in with a SWAT-type battering ram and make for the bed, I could give him a warm welcome.

It was a little strange, lying there with a weapon, and my thoughts moving inexorably toward Holly Samara and Sophie Montag. What was this? High school? Who to ask to the prom? Not as simple as that. Nothing's simple with you, Romeo. You're lying here hoping somebody comes after you, for crying out loud. People shoot at you. What kind of future would that be for a woman? *"Goodnight, honey, and don't mind the steel baton under the pillow."*

I fell into a restless sleep that was uninterrupted. Maybe the best I could hope for.

E ncino is tucked between Tarzana and Sherman Oaks. Before the lockdowns it had a thriving business corridor along Ventura. It was starting to show a little more life now, though there were still a lot of FOR LEASE signs posted up and down the boulevard. At ten o'clock in the morning there was some good activity going on outside the building I was scoping.

It was the biggest one in the area.

I parked Spinoza at a meter and popped the trunk. In a small duffel I had a few items courtesy of Ira Rosen, who had them courtesy of some old contacts with Mossad. One of these was a GPS tracker. The best and most compact GPS devices are made in Israel. These little beauties are the color and size of a junior league hockey puck, adhere via rare-earth magnets, and have the most advanced antennae in the world. I pocketed one, closed the trunk, and headed into the building.

The lobby directory had lawyers, dentists, various companies, a real estate brokerage, a lot of names and a few CPAs. Nothing there listing Verecundus Libri or Adrian Hart.

There was a back door to the parking garage. I went out and took a stroll around the tenant parking. It took up the entire lower level, and half the incline up to the next. That's where his car was. It was parked in a spot reserved for 661.

I attached the GPS tracker to the car's frame just inside the rear wheel well.

Back in the lobby I scanned the directory for 661, but didn't find the number.

I got in an elevator with a woman wearing a mask.

"Nice day," I said.

She looked away and stepped to the corner.

On the sixth floor I walked down the corridor to the end and found 661. There was a metal sign on the door—Accounting Office.

I gave it a knock.

And waited.

Another knock.

A woman's voice said, "Who is it?"

I said, "Package for Mr. Hart."

"Package?"

"Signature required."

The door opened. The woman was in her fifties, dressed for the office, with glasses on a chain around her neck.

I stepped in.

"Wait!" the woman said.

"I'm the package," I said. "You don't have to sign."

"You can't come in here!"

"Tell Mr. Hart that Mr. Romeo would like to see him."

"He doesn't see... he sees no one without an appointment. Please leave."

"He'll see me," I said.

She pulled herself up with authority. "Sir, if you don't—"

"It's all right, Linda." Adrian Hart was standing by the reception desk. He wore navy blue slacks, a white shirt and burgundy tie. His expression was hard yet serene, like an undertaker with a busy mortuary.

Linda gave me the stink eye as she answered her boss. "Are you sure?"

"Quite sure. This way, Mr. Romeo."

I stepped past Cerberus—I mean, Linda the Assistant—and followed Hart to his office. He closed the door.

"Please sit," he said,

I did. He sat behind a neat desk. Two computer monitors dominated the desk. A glass bowl with Hershey's Kisses and mini Mr. Goodbars sat on the corner nearest me. I resisted temptation.

As if I were a prospective client, he said, "What can I do for you?"

"Well, for starters, you can compensate me for some damaged petunias."

"Excuse me?"

"When you left your rent-a-thug behind, I had to subdue him and he ended up on top of my flowers."

"Are you being serious?"

"A hundred bucks, and we'll call it even."

"I don't have any intention of paying you anything, Mr. Romeo."

"That puzzles me," I said. "Since you came out to my place to threaten me."

"No, sir," he said. "I came to make a reasonable request."

"With Nick."

"He was with me purely for protection," he said. "Your reputation had preceded you."

I snorted. "That's a good one. You were the one who told him to go ahead."

"As I recall, you grabbed me and threatened me. Is that not correct?"

"You woke me up from a peaceful sleep."

"You are not a serious man," Hart said.

"How serious are you?" I said. "You took off as soon as Nick took over."

"I wanted no part of violence."

"You're a good liar," I said. "You might even be able to beat a machine."

"If the insults are over, you can leave now."

"The insults are just getting started," I said. "I haven't moved on to miscreant."

With a cool demeanor, Adrian Hart leaned back in his chair. "I don't imagine either of us has time for this."

"I have lots of time," I said.

"I don't," Adrian Hart said. "Anything else?"

"How did a guy like you hook up with a guy like San Dae-Ho?"

Not even a jaw clench from Adrian Hart. "You've done some homework."

"I was one of the few kids who liked homework."

Hart put his hands out. *So?*

"Here's some other self-study. Code name: Shy Book."

He blinked a couple of times without moving any other part of his body. "I'm sure I don't know what you mean."

"Verecundus Libri," I said.

"What?"

"Latin."

"Okay."

"A clever name for an accountant who likes to keep a low profile."

Finally, I got a reaction. His cheeks tightened. Not enough for a complete confession, but it would suffice for my purposes.

I said, "Low-profile accountants usually have clients who would like to remain off the books."

He leaned forward to say something. I heard a buzz. At least he said "Excuse me" as he looked at his phone. Apparently, a text.

He put the phone down on the desk. "Mr. Romeo, let's have a reasonable conversation, shall we? I know some things about you. I know that you are considered a very smart fellow. You can obviously fight. Those two things come into conflict with each other from time to time, wouldn't you say?"

"Are we doing psych profiles now?"

"Only tangentially," he said.

I couldn't help smiling. "Anybody who uses the word *tangentially* isn't exactly dumb."

"You're right about that. You may think you're the smartest one in the room, but perhaps not in this office. Where did you go to college?"

"Yale."

"Not bad. Stanford for me."

"Not bad yourself."

"I majored in Economics. Got a Masters at the University of Chicago."

"You should be teaching somewhere," I said. "Not hiding clients and money."

"So much you don't know," Hart said.

"Fill me in," I said.

"You present yourself as a man with a moral vision," Hart said. "That is quaint, but most outdated. There is no moral vision. There is only buying and selling, and always has been. Throughout history, however, the buying aspect was rarely by way of a free market. Buying was usually more via acquisition and conquest."

"True enough," I said.

"The Mongols, for example, once ruled the largest contiguous empire in the history of the world."

"Genghis Khan."

"Precisely. From this the Mongols facilitated trade and unprecedented exchange between east and west. Some argue they made possible the modern world."

"While slaughtering millions of people," I said.

"Which you would call immoral," Hart said. "Others would call it the cost of doing business."

"So you're going to tell me that hidden accounts and drug money laundering are just part of today's costs?"

He smiled. "Of course not, because that's a fantasy which you hold in your head. It is to tell you that you have no idea who you're dealing with, and the cost to you of further proceedings could get quite expensive. I trust I've made myself clear."

I stood. "I'd love to traipse through the lessons of history with you, but I don't have the time for it. Maybe when you're in prison I can come for a visit and we can chat some more about the rise and fall of empires."

"I'll show you out."

We walked back through the reception area.

Linda wasn't there.

I had ten minutes left on the meter. I would not be cheated! I put Spinoza's top down, got in and called Ira. I filled him in on the meeting and told him about the tracker. He said he'd run it through a program he'd designed that would collect the addresses of every stop that lasted over a minute.

Which meant a long wait before figuring out the next move. It was frustrating. I was in a cul-de-sac with the investigation. No one left to interview. I'd have to backtrack and try to shake something out of a tree I'd already pruned.

When the meter changed I waited another minute, just to squeeze a little extra time from the city. It owed me that. It owed all of us that. It had asked us to abide by rules and lockdowns and orders handed down from unelected bureaucrats with Robespierre Syndrome.

So yeah, a little bit of grace from my town was called for.

I decided to go to Jimmy's gym and work out. Maybe by late afternoon or evening Ira would have something on Adrian Hart's car. Maybe by punching the heavy bag I'd blast open a new thought or two.

There was mild traffic on Ventura.

Which made picking up the van following me easier.

It was dark blue with an illegally tinted windshield. I couldn't see the driver. But he was keeping a steady distance between himself and Spinoza. I increased the speed a bit. The van did too.

To confirm the tail, I made the standard move. I turned right at the next corner and headed into a residential area. The van followed. I took the next right on a side street. Ditto the van. One more right at the next corner, heading back to Ventura. The van stayed with me.

Now I knew, and the van knew I knew.

And at that precise moment it made its move.

Engine gunning, it moved into the next lane. It reached me just before I slowed so it would shoot past. Somehow, the van anticipated what I'd do. A real pro at the wheel.

And then something thunked into my back seat.

Something thrown from the van.

Which hit the gas and made for the boulevard.

I knew I had only seconds.

I jammed the brakes and burned rubber. Just before Spinoza was completely stopped I opened the door and jumped out, heading across the street.

Halfway across I heard the explosion.

Something hard and hot hit me in the left calf. I stumbled forward, conking my head on the curb.

. . .

Y ou're lying stunned and bloody on a street, you expect
     maybe the next car to stop and offer to help a fellow
human being in some distress. Instead, I heard a honk as a
car swerved around me and kept on its merry way. I was
conscious enough to crawl out of the street and onto the
sidewalk. Woozy, on my back, I felt my calf. Blood covered
my hand. A chunk of flesh was missing, as was a portion of
my jeans.

Somebody said, "What was that?"

I looked up and saw a woman outside the door of a
house. She looked at me with fear in her eyes, and who
could blame her these days?

"I'm hurt," I said. "Can you call—"

She scurried back inside and slammed the door.

Across the street, where Spinoza was, a man with gray
hair and an ample belly looked angrily at the convertible in
front of his house. Then around, as if searching for the
driver. He spotted me.

"Hey, what's going on?" he said.

I struggled to my feet. My calf burned. "Can you call the
police?" I said.

"This your car?" he said.

"Yes. Can you call—"

"You drunk?"

"Police. Call the police."

"What?"

I started limping across the street, leaving a trail of
blood spots.

The man backed up.

When I got to Spinoza I was afraid of what I'd see, like
getting to a wounded soldier on a machine-gunned
battlefield.

It was bad.

The seats in back were ripped apart. There was a ragged hole on the driver's side. Shards of shrapnel were embedded everywhere.

The man was looking at me from his porch. He had his phone to his ear.

I unlocked the trunk. I took out the first aid kit and wiped down my wound with a couple of antiseptic towelettes, then wrapped gauze around my calf and taped it.

The man said, "I called 911."

"Thanks," I said.

"What happened?"

"I'm not sure," I said.

"I mean, look at your car."

"I know," I said.

"Did something explode?"

"Yeah."

"Like what?"

"If you don't mind, let's wait for the police," I said.

"Sure," he said. "Can I get you a bottle of water or something?"

"That'd be great."

I sat on the curb and called Ira.

"There's been a little setback," I said.

"Oh dear," Ira said.

"Somebody tossed an exploding device in my car."

Pause.

"When?"

"Just now. While I was driving."

"Michael! Are you hurt?"

"A rip in the leg, not too bad, but Spinoza's in bad shape."

"Where are you? Can I come get you?"

"Encino. The cops will be here soon."

"Who did this?"

"I don't know. A van was following me. But I have more than a sneaking suspicion that Adrian Hart had something to do with it."

"Why?"

"He started talking in his office. He was stalling. Enough time for his assistant to get a message out to somebody."

"Did you get a plate on the van?"

"It didn't have a front plate," I said.

"Give me an address. I'm coming to get you."

I looked across the street and read the number on the house.

"I'll be there as soon as I can," Ira said.

T he man came back and handed me a bottle of water.

"That's very neighborly of you," I said.

"That's a funny thing to say."

"It is?"

"You don't look like somebody who'd say that."

I opened the water and took a drink.

"You live around here?" he said.

"Paradise Cove," I said.

"You're a long way from home."

"Don't I know it."

"You don't seem to be worried about the police," he said.

"I don't have any reason to be."

"Things like this don't happen in our neighborhood," he said. "Nearest thing was some kids shot off fireworks in the street last Fourth of July and set one of the pine trees on fire."

A few neighbors were out now, surveying the scene. I stayed on the curb. I was there when the black-and-white arrived a few minutes later.

T he officer who questioned me—a thirty-something man named Congreve—had an incredulous look I couldn't blame him for. I laid it all out, described the van as best I could.

"We'll have the car towed to the station so forensics can have a look," Congreve said.

"Take good care of him," I said.

"Of who?"

"My car. His name is Spinoza, and I want to save him. Treat him gently."

"It... he looks pretty bad."

"Just keep him safe until I can get him back."

Congreve smiled a little. "Now about your leg. You should have it looked at. We can take you—"

"Not necessary," I said.

"You sure?"

Ira's van was coming slowly toward us.

"I'm sure," I said.

I introduced Ira to the officers. He gave them his information and said I would be staying with him until further notice. He worked in some legal mumbo jumbo to protect my interests.

Then the tow truck arrived. I got the duffel from the trunk before they hooked up Spinoza. As they drove him off I thought I saw his taillights flicker with fear and trembling.

"Let's get you home," Ira said.

"The Cove?" I said.

"My house."

"I don't want to bring trouble to your house," I said.

"We'll be ready for it," Ira said.

Good enough for me. Truth be told, I wanted to be with Ira. He's my rock. It's been that way ever since that time in Nashville when I saw him, in his wheelchair, being accosted by some teen thugs. I took care of the thugs. From then on, Ira began to take care of me.

We went to the Motel 6 where I gathered my stuff and checked out.

On the way to Ira's, he said, "You need a few days' rest."

"We can't afford that," I said.

"I'll do the assessing."

"Maybe I need to get out of this place."

"L.A.?"

"California. Go someplace where there's no trouble at all."

"There is such a place," Ira said.

"Yeah?"

"It's not a place you can get to by a boat or a train. It's someplace far, far away, behind the moon—"

"All right, stop."

"There's no place like home, Michael."

"I could become a monk," I said.

"It's not in you," Ira said. "You're a scale balancer."

"A what?"

"You have to balance the scales. It's what drives you."

"I'm tired of being driven," I said.

"You also wouldn't make it as a hermit," Ira said. "Despite what you think, you need people in your life."

"Do I?"

"Me," Ira said. "You'd be a sad case if you didn't have me around, wouldn't you say?"

He was right about that. But I flippantly said, "So sad."

"And that young man you're helping in Paradise Cove. What's his name? Dog something?"

"C Dog."

"You're making a positive difference there."

"Maybe," I said.

"What about Sophie?" Ira said.

"Don't ask me about her."

"And this DEA agent?"

"Or about her."

"And then there's—"

"Don't talk about anything," I said. "Just drive."

A t Ira's he assessed my wound. "You'll have a nice scar," he said. "It'll be like a divot on a golf course."

He patched it up fresh, then said, "Grab a book and go outside and read for awhile."

"I don't want to read," I said. "I don't want to think. I'm tired of thinking. What can I do to not think?"

"There's always TV."

"Perfect," I said. "One of those old sitcoms. How about *Gilligan's Island?*"

"I can't allow that," Ira said. "There is down time, and there is melt-your-brain time."

"A little brain melt might be nice."

"How about an old movie? *Sunset Boulevard, Stalag 17, All About Eve?*"

"Dramas?"

"Or comedy. *Some Like it Hot, Duck Soup.*"

"Marx Brothers."

"That's the ticket," Ira said. "I have the DVD."

He set me up in his den. I sat in his recliner and got nice

and comfortable. He put in the DVD of *Duck Soup* and said, "I'm right here if you need anything."

The movie started up. Intrigue in the land of Freedonia. They were expecting a new leader, one Rufus T. Firefly. Groucho, of course. He comes on scene with soldiers holding up their swords in anticipation. He joins them and holds up his cigar.

Then Mrs. Teasdale, played by the redoubtable Margaret Dumont, spots him. "Oh, Your Excellency, we've been expecting you. As chairwoman of the reception committee, I extend to you the good wishes of every man, woman and child of Freedonia."

"Never mind that stuff," says Groucho, spreading a deck of cards. "Take a card."

"Eh? What'll I do with the card?"

"You can keep it. I've got fifty-one left."

I smiled. A good sign. And I kept that smile as Rufus T. Firefly is introduced to a beautiful dancer, who proposes they dance together sometime.

"I could dance with you till the cows come home," he says. "On second thought, I'd rather dance with the cows till you come home."

At which point Ira said, "You may want to look at this."

"I'm watching the movie," I said.

"Michael..."

Groaning, I got up and trundled to his living room office. He pointed at the monitor. It showed a map of the Valley. Two red dots blinked at disparate locations. A blue dot blinked and was on the move.

"Hart," I said.

"He's stopped at two locations, and is on his way to another."

"Now I have to think," I said.

"Good to have you back." He hit a key and a box with

two addresses popped up. Ira clicked on the first, and a Google street view photo appeared.

A gas station.

He clicked the second. The address was in the rural residential area called Box Canyon, at the west end of the San Fernando Valley. The photo showed a house of eclectic design. It may have once been an inviting Spanish hacienda, but now it was more neo-biker what with the overgrown weeds and a Harley parked in the driveway.

I said, "Can you find out who owns the place?"

"Give me a minute."

He clacked away. In under sixty seconds he found a page with the property listing, its dimensions, date of build (1964) and title holder. Someone named Paul Jenkins.

"He bought the place in '97," Ira said.

"What can we find out about him?"

"It's a common name. I can try some cross checks."

"You do that. I'm going back to Groucho."

Which is what I did. Rufus T. Firefly called his cabinet meeting to order. A minister says, "Your Excellency, here is the Treasury Department's report. I hope you find it clear."

"Clear?" says Firefly. "Why a four-year-old child could understand this report." He leans over to his secretary and mutters, "Run out and find me a four-year-old child, I can't make head or tail out of it."

It struck me that this could very well be mistaken as a documentary about California politics.

"It's a rental," Ira said.

I went back to the office. "This is no way for me to watch—"

"Paul Jenkins is the owner, but the place is a rental. It's been that for a long time."

"Wait a second," I said. "Go to the street view again."

Ira returned to the photo of the house in Box Canyon.

"Click on the timeline," I said.

Ira put the cursor on the little clock icon, and brought up the street view timeline. The photo we were looking at had been taken five months ago.

"Click on the one before that," I said.

He did. It was taken over a year earlier.

"How about that?" I said. The photo showed the house, only this time a blue van with tinted windows was in the driveway.

"Is that the van?" Ira said.

"It has to be. And now we have a Hart connection."

"Good," Ira said.

"Let's see where Mr. Hart is now."

Ira went back to the GPS map. The blue dot was heading south, nearing Ventura Boulevard in the Studio City area.

"How about Tibet?" I said.

"Hm?" Ira said.

"I could move to Tibet and become a holy man. People can come to me and ask for the secret to life."

"And what will you tell them?"

"I'll think of something," I said.

"Stay with me," Ira said. "You'll do less damage."

We watched the dot. It crossed Ventura and proceeded up a street, took a turn.

And stopped.

We waited until that dot turned red.

"Let's have a look," Ira said.

He brought up the street view.

"I know that house," I said. "It's where Bianca Aiken lives."

"Remind me."

"She's the girl who broke up with Clint and goes around with Gavin McGuane now. I started talking to her, then her father showed up. He got a little pushy."

"So what might be his connection with Hart?"

"Can you get the title?"

"Sure."

Ira brought up the property listing.

"It was bought five years ago," Ira said. "The name on the title is Timothy Aiken."

"Why don't we drive out there and have a meet up with them?"

"Uh-uh," Ira said. "We don't have enough connective tissue yet."

"Then let's deep dive," I said.

Which is done through Ira and his self-designed search engine. With a few keystrokes we had some pages about Timothy Aiken.

A LinkedIn profile was on top. It listed Timothy Aiken as a "serial entrepreneur and private equity investor with expertise in digital commerce, digital currency, crypto currency, entertainment media and telecommunications industry experience."

"Crypto currency," I said. "Media. Not exactly sure bets for a serial entrepreneur."

"Let's have a look at his entertainment presence."

Ira clacked over to IMDb, the Internet Movie Database, and typed "Timothy Aiken" in the search box.

No results found for "timothy aiken"

"Well," I said, "at least he talks a good game."

"Let's see what else we can find," Ira said, and started finding.

I sat and watched the master at work. After sixty seconds or so he said, "Looks like he went to high school out in the Valley. Reseda High. Here's a yearbook photo."

Indeed, there it was. A senior photo of a young, unsmiling Timothy Aiken.

"The whole yearbook is online," Ira said. "You want to flip through it?"

"And see if he was in Chess Club?"

"Michael, our currency is information. Every bit helps."

"Let's roll," I said.

We flipped the pages and found Timothy Aiken on the baseball team.

And the History Club. This was a group photo, with six students and a teacher wearing costumes. A girl was decked out like Marie Antoinette. One of the boys was a cowboy. The teacher wore a white wig and blue uniform, a la George Washington.

Our boy Timothy was dressed in an Army uniform of World War II vintage.

"You thinking what I'm thinking?" Ira said.

"Military fan," I said.

"This yearbook came out half a year after the 9/11 attack."

"Can we find out if he enlisted?"

"Military service records are kept at the National Personnel Records Center in St. Louis, and are private."

"What about FOIA?"

"Yes, the Freedom of Information Act applies. Limited access, though, unless approved by next of kin."

"Can we get anything?" I said.

"If he served, we can get his final duty status, assignments, decorations, things like that."

"How long does it take?"

"You have to submit a request, in writing. Of course..."

"Go on," I said.

"I can make another request, to one of my contacts in intelligence."

"It's helpful to have a network," I said.

"You have no idea," he said. "Go finish your movie."

. . .

That's what I did. Freedonia wins its war with Sylvania, and the Marx Brothers pelt the villain Trentino with fruit. Mrs. Teasdale begins singing the Freedonia National Anthem, in her bellows-like voice, and the boy begins pelting *her* with the fruit.

The End.

And I was refreshed, ready to put Groucho Marx in charge of the city. My leg divot was sore and itchy but I was in otherwise fine shape.

Ira called me in. He'd prepared some tea and insisted I take a cup.

"A calming tea," Ira said.

"I am most serene," I said.

"There are things you are most of," Ira said. "Serene is not one of them."

"Say that to me again and I'll tear this office apart."

"Sit," he said.

He showed me the monitor. "Timothy Aiken's service record."

A form on the screen showed several boxes.

The first showed service in Iraq and Afghanistan.

The second listed a Good Conduct Medal.

The third was the most interesting: Qualified Sharp-shooter, M24.

"That's our shooter," I said.

"Circumstantial evidence," Ira said.

"Strong circumstantial evidence," I said. "Let's confront him with it."

"Easy. We form a theory of the case first, then build on it."

I got up. Went to the window. Looked out. The day was

overcast. Like me, the city needed clarity. We both needed light.

Ira was working the keyboard again when something flashed in my brain.

"T," I said.

"You want more tea?" Ira said.

I turned around. "The letter T. Timothy. The letter B, Bianca. What if the T and B in Clint's drawing was for them?"

Ira swiveled around. "Could be."

"There's your theory of the case," I said. "Bianca is involved in selling cheating materials at Elias. What if she was also a moving part in the drug traffic? Daddy running the show, with enforcement help from Adrian Hart."

"It's a good theory. Now we need evidence."

"Let's have a look inside Aiken's house," I said.

"And how are you going to do that?" Ira said.

"Let myself in," I said.

Ira rubbed the bridge of his nose.

"After all," I said, "that's not a crime."

"You're too clever for your own good," Ira said.

"But I'm right, right? It's not burglary, because I don't have the intent to steal anything. And it's not trespass, because I don't intend to occupy the place for any length of time. Tell me I'm wrong."

"It's quite true that the penal code requires you have the specific intent to interfere with another's property rights, and that you actually did so interfere."

"If I'm there for a short time, have a look see, and get out, it's not trespass."

"I assume you're going to do your lock-picking skills to get in the door."

"Sounds good to me," I said. "If I get dinged for breaking and entering, I can take it."

"As much as it pains me to correct you," Ira said, "there is no crime in California called 'breaking and entering.' That's for the TV shows."

"So I'm good," I said.

"What about the security system? It's sure to be sophisticated."

"That's where you come in," I said.

"Oh, I do?"

"That's your meat. So what do you suggest?"

"I suggest we knock on the door and politely ask to speak with him."

"I love this plan," I said. "And plan B is we break in and I mess him up some."

"There will be no plan B, Michael."

"We'll see."

We took Ira's van toward Studio City.

"Strategy," Ira said. "If he is home, he will likely not immediately open the door to us. We must coax him to do so."

"You have a suggestion?"

"We tell him we've come about Bianca, that we have some information we need to discuss."

"Good," I said. "One of my rules is that we don't owe the truth to those who lie."

"We are not lying," Ira said.

"Then we're withholding the whole truth," I said.

"Exactly," Ira said. "After all, God did the same thing."

"Beg pardon?"

"When God rejected Saul as King of Israel, he told the prophet Samuel to go to the house of Jesse, where he would reveal the new king, which would be David. Samuel said he was afraid Saul would find out and try to kill him. God told

Samuel to take a heifer with him, and say that he had come to offer a sacrifice. This was true, but not the whole truth, and it prevented potential evil."

"We have no cow," I said. "But we do have info on Bianca."

"That's it."

"And if he doesn't open the door?" I said.

"We tell him we will return with the police," Ira said.

"Will the police come with us?"

"I have the power of persuasion," Ira said.

"And if he does let us in?"

"We begin slowly to close the net. At some point, a netted animal will strike. He will make some move, at which point you will subdue him."

"I like that part," I said.

"This will be purely out of self-defense," Ira said.

I smiled.

Ira said, "Just remember, the law requires you may only use the degree of force reasonably necessary under the circumstances. Don't get too enthusiastic. Just control. And once that happens, we will conduct a search of the house."

"Can we do that?" I said.

"We are not law enforcement," Ira said. "We will be operating under our own authority. Anything we find can be turned over to the police, who may rightfully use it."

"And if we don't find anything?"

"Timothy Aiken could threaten to sue us. But he won't. Unless he's stupid, and I don't believe he is. Dangerous, but not stupid."

"What if he has a weapon?"

"He won't when he lets us inside," Ira said. "We keep an eye on him. We do our talking standing up."

. . .

W e stopped a little way down the street from the
    Aiken house. We could see most of it, including
the driveway. Timothy Aiken's black Escalade was parked
there.

Ira got his forearm crutches from behind the seat and
said, "Ready?"

"Let's go, Wyatt," I said.

"Who?"

"I'm Doc Holliday."

"This is not the O.K. Corral," Ira said, "and it's best you
not think of it that way."

"I'm your huckleberry," I said, and got out of the van.
I'm sure Ira sighed, but I didn't hear him.

We walked up to the front door. Same door, same
camera as the first time I was here. I knocked, waited,
knocked again.

A voice inside said, "What do you want?"

"We need to talk, Mr. Aiken," Ira said.

"I told him I had nothing to say," Aiken said.

"There's more information now," Ira said. "This
shouldn't take long."

"No," Timothy Aiken said.

"I'm a lawyer," Ira said. "The information concerns your
daughter."

Pause.

Then a click, and the door opened.

Timothy Aiken was barefoot, dressed in black jeans and
a red golf shirt, untucked.

"What about Bianca?" he said.

"Mind if we come in?" I said.

"Yeah, I do," Timothy said.

"Thanks," I said, and pushed the door open all the way
and stepped past him.

"Hey!" Aiken said.

"Michael!" Ira said.

I got behind Aiken so he was between me and Ira.

"You don't mind if I have a look around, do you?" I said.

"Got out of my house!" Aiken said.

"Please excuse this idiot," Ira said. "Michael, just stay where you are."

The clever rabbi came in.

"I don't want either one of you here," Aiken said.

"Two minutes of your time," Ira said. "Can we sit?"

"No," Aiken said. "Say what you're going to say and leave."

"Very well," Ira said.

"Let me," I said.

"Calm yourself, Michael. Mr. Aiken, I am Ira Rosen, an attorney representing Clint Cunningham. You already know my blunderbuss, Mr. Romeo."

"Yeah," Aiken said. "What about my daughter?"

Ira said, "Yes, well, I do not wish to see anyone of her age caught up in something that could ruin the rest of her life."

"Like what?" Aiken said.

"For example, selling cheating materials to school-mates," Ira said.

"How would you know that?" Aiken said.

I raised my hand. "I caught her and her boyfriend *in flagrante delicto*."

"In what?" Aiken said.

"Blazing offense," I said. "Red-handed. Selling tests and papers to another student."

"We also need to explore another connection," Ira said. "One that does not seem entirely random."

Aiken tried to keep his demeanor angry, but he was

starting to look nervous. His eyes did a little darting around.

Ira said, "Specifically, your connection to a Mr. Adrian Hart."

Aiken paused. "Who?"

"The gentleman who visited you today."

"I have no idea what you're talking about," Aiken said.

I said, "You're in this up to your eyeballs, Aiken, and we're going to prove it and take you down, and your daughter, too. Because I think you—"

"Michael," Ira said

"—pimped her out to Clint Cunningham, set him up as a fall guy, and then scared him so bad he's afraid to talk. You and Hart are running drugs at Elias. And one more thing. You took out a cop with a rifle shot meant for me. Not too good for an Army sharpshooter such as yourself."

His eyes signaled his next move. I'd seen it a hundred times in the cage. Read the eyes, control the man.

He made a dash toward the innards of his house.

All I had to do was stick out my good leg and trip him.

He went sprawling on the hardwood floor.

Which is when I looked up at the staircase.

And saw Bianca Aiken, pointing a 9 mil at me.

"Stop!" Bianca said.

The gun was unsteady in her hand.

And her finger was on the trigger.

Timothy Aiken got to his knees. He was about to jump up.

I dipped and wrapped my arm around his throat. I pulled him up, making him a human shield between me and the girl with the gun.

"Let him go!" Bianca said.

Ira spoke with calm authority. "Put the gun down, Bianca. No one will get hurt."

The girl seemed on the verge of tears when she repeated, "Let him go!"

"Take your finger off the trigger, Bianca," I said.

"Let's talk this through," Ira said.

Bianca turned the gun on Ira.

"It's all right," Ira said. "We're not here to hurt anybody."

Timothy struggled against my hold, but he wasn't going anywhere.

"You're going to kill us!" Bianca said.

"No one dies today," I said. "Just take your finger off the trigger and point the gun down."

Bianca only did the second thing.

Which is why the gun went off.

A trigger-finger twitch happens when there's too much stress coursing through your nerves. It's involuntary, and any movement can set it off. When Bianca, almost crying, lowered the gun, her finger pulled the trigger.

Blam... and a bullet splintered the stairs.

Bianca screamed, slipped backward, the gun came up.

Another shot fired.

It tore into Timothy Aiken's chest.

Bianca screamed again, louder, and dropped the gun.

"Daddy!" She scrambled down the remaining stairs.

I let go of Aiken's neck and lowered him to the floor. His mouth flapped open and closed as he sought breath. Blood spurted from his chest.

Dropping to her knees, Bianca put her hands on her father's shirt. Her pitiful wail cut the air.

Ira went to his knees and pushed Bianca out of the way. "Take her," he said to me. "And call 911."

I lifted Bianca off her father. She writhed and screamed.

I carried the package into the living room. I sat in a chair and held her on my lap, my arms wrapped around her.

"Easy, easy, your dad will be looked after," I said. "Ira knows what he's doing. Okay? I'm calling 911. Okay?"

She made a last twitch, then relaxed. I kept my left arm around her, got my phone with my right. I called 911 and made the report.

Bianca went completely limp.

She'd passed out.

I picked her up and laid her on the sofa. There was a throw blanket there. I pulled it over her.

I went back to Ira. He was pressing on Aiken's chest with both hands.

"Towels, anything," he said.

I looked for the nearest bathroom. Got two towels off the rack and came back. Ira applied them and pressed down again.

"Where's the girl?" he asked.

"Passed out," I said.

"Keep an eye on her," Ira said.

I sat with her, glad she was out. She was going to need a lot of help after this. I hoped she'd get the right people on it. So much bad psych out there, trendy theories, bogus practices—if any real attention was paid at all. Gertrude Stein called Hemingway's generation "lost," simply because they were drifting through Paris, drinking and chattering. Bianca's generation was not just lost, but damaged. Betrayed by her father into a scheme like this one. And now facing the prospect of having killed him. Poor kid. Poor, poor kid.

. . .

Paramedics and cops came on scene. A good, sympathetic female officer took Bianca under her wing. Timothy Aiken was put on a gurney and wheeled out. Ira spoke to another officer.

I backed away and started looking around while I had the chance. As Ira said, anything found could be used as evidence, as I was not law enforcement. But my window of time was short.

The stairway was where the activity was, so I stayed on the ground floor. The kitchen, the laundry room, a door to the garage.

I went through it.

Looked around. Neat, with shelves and tools. A cooler. Nothing in it but frozen meat and chicken and assorted items, like mint chip ice cream and Newman's Own Thin & Crispy Pizzas.

There were three cabinets on one wall. They held paint cans, bleach, weed killer, tools, electric wire, rope. As I was not redesigning a house, I left all this and went back inside.

The spacious living room had a bar with a granite top. Behind it was a full-on liquor shelf that would have done a mid-size restaurant proud. A classic place to store a weapon is underneath a bar top, so I came around and had a look. No guns.

Turning, I had a look at the liquor shelf. Well stocked, with a preference for vodka and bourbon. The shelf stuck out from the wall about eight inches and had four levels. I took a peek under the bottom shelf, another place a weapon might be hidden. Nothing there.

Except a padlock.

Now that was interesting. It was a heavy-duty lock in the bottom corner. It was through a latch which you couldn't see unless you looked right at it.

It was crying out to me to be picked.

There is one padlock that's nearly impossible to pick, the Bowley. It's been done, but only with the right tools and plenty of time. This wasn't a Bowley, so my Joey Feint lock-pick kit would do the trick.

It took me one minute to pop the lock.

When I did, the entire liquor shelf moved an inch. I stood and pulled it open.

Behind it was a cache of guns.

Six handguns. A shotgun.

And one sniper rifle. A Remington 700, complete with a long-range scope.

"Hey, what're you doing there?"

A detective, from the look of him—shield worn on his belt—had come upon my little enterprise.

"I'm saving you time," I said.

He was a sinewy man in his fifties with the suspicious look of an LAPD lifer. But his look went from suspicion to interest as he came closer and saw the weapons.

"Don't touch anything," he said.

"My name's Romeo," I said. "I work for the lawyer, Ira Rosen. We came here to talk to Aiken and no doubt you heard what happened."

"What made you think you could search the place?"

"The fact that I'm a private citizen," I said. "And took no direction from you. I suggest you get ballistics on this Remington and see if there's a match with the slug they took out of an LAPD officer named Aoki. Talk to an SID investigator named Monica Helberg."

The detective took out his phone and snapped a pic of the weapons.

"I have some questions for you," the detective said.

"I have some answers," I said.

. . .

So did Ira, who handled the whole aftermath with his usual panache. Which is why I kept my tongue in check as much as I could. It is sometimes possible.

Our next stop was at the LAPD station in the Valley where Spinoza was in the trauma ward, otherwise known as a corner of the parking lot. The officer who'd had Spinoza brought in, Congreve, was there.

"Nothing to report yet," he said. "It's going to take awhile."

"We have something to report," I said. "Has an investigator been assigned to this yet?"

"That'd be Detective Palsberg," Congreve said. "You want to talk to him?"

"He'll want to talk to us," I said.

"Have a seat."

Ronald Palsberg had career-division written all over him. Meaning he'd made detective but never got to Robbery-Homicide Division, the elite squad downtown. But often these local guys are the ones who do the best grunt work, which is sometimes taken away from them by an RHD guy with eyes on good publicity or political leverage.

Palsberg had a veteran paunch and a friendly demeanor. His hair was close cropped and the color of unpolished handcuffs. He wore a mask.

We did the introductions and laid out our common ground. He wanted to take us inside for an interview, but I said, "I know who did it, and where we can find him."

I explained why.

"My partner's out for the day," Palsberg said. "I can at least go ask a few questions."

"I suggest you go with backup," I said.

B ox Canyon is a hilly, rocky, scrubby, hot and inhospitable slice of earth between L.A. and Ventura Counties. A haven for snakes, coyotes, skunks, possums and the occasional bobcat. They used to shoot a lot of TV Westerns there because it was so close to Hollywood. It wasn't much for homes except for a few hermit types in shacks.

Then the hippies of the 1960s discovered it. And gradually, actual houses began to spring up, spaced well apart and of no common design. More than a few bikers came to call the place home, too. Some of the roads snaking around the place aren't paved.

That was the case of the San Dae-Ho pad. Palsberg rode with two officers in a black-and-white. Ira and I followed in Ira's van. We stopped thirty yards from the house.

Palsberg got out and came to Ira's window.

"That the van?" he asked.

"It is," I said.

"Stay here," he said. "If I need you for anything I'll let you know."

He went back to the black-and-white. Then he and two male officers started up the road.

"What do you think?" I asked Ira.

"He knows what he's doing," Ira said. "He'll ask some questions, then ask if he can take a look in the van. If San Dae-Ho says no, he'll try to get a warrant."

"Try?"

"Your statement is a thin reed for probable cause. But he and the officers will be on the alert for anything in plain view that might point to possible criminal activity."

"Can they look in the garage?"

"Not unless it's open and viewable from the driveway. Officers can approach a house and anything they can see is fair game."

"Can they look through the windows of the van?"

"Probably," Ira said. "There was a case out of the Ninth Circuit where DEA agents looked through the tinted windows of a parked van at a 7-Eleven. It held there was a lesser expectation of privacy for a van in a public place, even with tinted windows. The difference here is that the van is parked on a private driveway. It'd be safer to get a warrant."

"You're the smartest man in this van," I said.

"High praise," Ira said.

I looked up the road. Couldn't see Palsberg or the officers. They were probably at the door. They were probably talking right now to—

—not San Dae-Ho.

"There he goes," I said.

He was scurrying up into the hills from the back of the house.

I jumped out of the van.

"Michael!" Ira said.

I ignored him. I ignored the pain in my leg, too, and ran up to the house where the cop trio was walking back to the road.

"He's up there," I said. "He ran out."

Palsberg looked up, without concern. "We'll come back."

"Who knows if he'll be here?" I said. "Let's go."

"We have no cause to stop him," Palsberg said.

"I do," I said, and started around the house.

"Come back here!" Palsberg said.

I ignored him, too.

. . .

H e scampered up further into the hills. Nothing up there but big boulders and crags and places to hide. Somebody who lived here had the advantage of knowing where to hide.

In ancient warfare it was not uncommon for armies to send solo warriors into the field for a mano a mano. This was usually preceded by a lot of shouting and trash talk.

I like the ancient ways. So to keep San Dae-Ho in sight I started throwing shade.

I began with the coward card, always a good opening salvo. "Hey Shorty! You afraid to fight? I heard you were good. All I see is your butt running away."

For a moment I lost sight of him behind a big rock. Which is where he stayed.

Was he listening?

"No police around," I said. "Just you and me. End it now so I don't have to hunt you down and cut off your ponytail."

I looked down and saw Palsberg and the cops talking to Ira.

"Better hurry," I said. "Looks like the cops may be on their way."

A slight wind through the canyon was the only sound. I took a few steps forward, stopping on a sun-bleached boulder.

"It's over for you, bud. We know about Adrian Hart. We know about everything. You could help yourself by copping—"

He jumped up from behind the rocks. Literally. It was a move few people could do. But with his compact size and springy legs he made it look easy.

He was smiling.

He had very white teeth.

There we were, like a couple of rams facing each other over a section of hill.

"I'm gonna gouge your eyes out," San Dae-Ho said.

"You, sir, are an uncircumcised Philistine."

He frowned. Good. I always like to stimulate thought.

"Tell you what," I said. "I'll let you live. But I'm going to break both your legs—one for Nick, and one for my car."

"Nick deserved it," he said. "Now you're gonna get what you deserve."

"I'm waiting," I said.

He dove at me like a hawk bearing down on a field mouse. It's normally bad technique to leave your feet in a fight—unless you can make the move San Dae-Ho did. I still don't know how he pulled it off. He bent his torso backward and shot his feet out. He had somehow done a one-eighty in the air. And even though I moved it was like he anticipated that's what I'd do. His right foot caught me flush on the head. I stumbled right and almost fell off my rock into a crevice. I managed to regain my footing but he was on me in a second.

He was fast. His fists flew. He was a taekwondo guy for sure, using speed and power to try and overwhelm.

I was only whelmed. I countered with a Jimmy Sarducci one-two. The one was my left jab, the two was a right cross that clapped him in the temple.

He was dazed for only a second. When I went in to clap him again, he leaned back a couple of inches and avoided my punch.

What came next was the fastest roundhouse kick I've ever seen. It rammed into my left thigh so hard it crunched the femoral nerve. My leg went numb and turned to jelly.

Though it was that jelly that saved me from his next strike, as I went down just as his kick whizzed over my head.

I knew another kick in fast-strike style was only a second away. But neural signals are faster. My right leg was still good. I fell backward and shot out my trusty heel. West met East in the valley of the nuts.

San Dae-Ho grunted and bent forward.

In the instant that followed I rolled and got to my feet. Or rather, foot. My left, attached to my numb leg, was of no use. It gave me only limited stability, as if one leg of a wooden stool had been zapped by a wizard and turned into warm butter.

At least I could push off with my right.

San Dae-Ho got back to his stance in the narrow Korean style.

Then he pounced.

I was sure he would kick again and aimed a Romeo's Hammer at the meat of his thigh. But he fooled me and came over the top with a full-on right cross to my face.

Down I went.

This time into the crevice.

W hat I thought as I fell is, I've been here before. Wedged in rocks. It happened once when I was in the Nevada desert and I almost didn't make it out. Some sort of instinct kicked in now, got me to turn my body and use my right arm like a shock absorber. I managed to keep from getting stuck, but I was still between a rock and a hard face—the face of San Dae-Ho looking down at me and enjoying the moment.

Which could be my last one. I couldn't stand the thought that this is how I'd go. In that flash of a moment what came to my mind were faces—of Ira and Sophie and C Dog and Holly. All jumbled together but somehow distinct.

And as San Dae-Ho jumped, his feet aimed at my face, I

pushed with my elbows with all the strength I had and turned my head, just enough to avoid a full strike. His feet grazed the back of my head and hit the round hardness of a boulder. That caused him to slip. He fell behind me.

Without looking, without having to look, I rammed my elbow where I knew his face would be.

And it was.

I flipped myself over and saw him groggy and trying to get up.

The back of his head was toward me.

I grabbed his ponytail and yanked his head back, hard.

Then gave him three lefts to the nose, *bam bam bam*.

The Korean skull has a wide, heart-shaped nasal aperture, which means more room for cartilage to be pounded back inside the head, causing all sorts of trauma, including blacking out.

San Dae-Ho was asleep. Which was good for him when I pulled his legs over the crevice so they formed a little bridge, with the knees in the very middle. I climbed up to the high spot where San Dae-Ho had been a moment before.

I was going to jump and break his legs. I was feeling it— the brute, the animal. He deserved it.

Ira, Sophie, C Dog, Holly.

I couldn't do it. Just couldn't.

I dragged his body out of the crevice and onto the side of the hill. There was a little footpath there, beaten into the sun-hardened dirt. I put him on it and started him down like a rolled-up carpet. I had to push him a few times with my foot. He tumbled over rocks and scrub. He finished about fifty yards from where his house was.

That's when Palsberg saw me and hurried over.

"Good God, what did you do to him?" he said.

"Self-defense," I said. "And by the way, he copped to killing Nick."

"Who's Nick?"

"I'll fill you in," I said. "And it'll get you that search warrant."

I t did. Paramedics took San Dae-Ho away. The telephonic warrant came in for Palsberg. They found three grenades in the van.

It was starting to get dark. Ira wrapped things up with Palsberg. Then we headed back to Ira's. We didn't say much. Ira knows when to get me to talk, and when not to.

This was a not to.

O n Friday we brought Clint home to his mother. The D.A. agreed to drop the charges in exchange for Clint's statement and testimony against Timothy Aiken— who unbelievably was going to make it. Clint was still scared, but knowing Aiken was going down helped a little.

Still, he was going to need time, lots of time, to climb out of the dark hole he was in. Trista told me she was going to take Clint out of Elias and have him finish up high school online. Then maybe she could find an art school for him to attend. I told her I thought that was a good idea.

On Saturday I got possession of Spinoza. I had him towed to an auto body shop run by one of Ira's former clients, Keith Johnson. The nice thing about it was that Johnson loved to restore classic cars. He had one, a beautiful 1959 Ford Fairlane, that he took to car shows. He told me it would be a long healing process, but thought he could restore my ride.

"And faintly trust the largest hope," I said.

"Huh?" Johnson said.

"Tennyson," I said.

"Huh?"

"The poet."

"Oh. Yeah."

To fill the automotive void—which one must do when his car's in the shop in L.A.—I rented a Ford Mustang of recent vintage. Spinoza would have approved. I drove over to Ira's Saturday evening, where he made me his famous matzo ball soup.

After finishing one of the delicious, schmaltz-laden spheres I looked at Ira and said, "There's something not right."

"With you?" Ira said.

"That goes without saying. I mean about this whole thing."

"Explain."

"I don't see Timothy Aiken and his daughter as master-minds of a drug enterprise in the Valley. At most they were agents. Franchisees. They take their share, but kick most of it up the line, through Adrian Hart, wherever he may be."

"You think Hart is the head of the snake?"

I shook my head. "He's the neck. Do snakes have necks?"

"Only vertebrae. A lot of vertebrae. Two hundred to four hundred."

"Okay, then he's the top ten vertebrae. But the Valley turf for Vector Dust is far and wide."

"But where Clint is concerned, the case is closed. So is our part in it."

I said nothing.

"What is it, Michael?"

"The scales aren't balanced," I said.

With a sigh, Ira said, "Shall I try to talk you out of it?"

I shook my head.

"What do you propose to do?" Ira said.

"Take another look inside Aiken's house," I said.

"Whatever for?"

"I wasn't finished looking around."

"May I remind you that it is a crime scene?"

"*Was* a crime scene. He had a hidden gun case. I want to see if he has a wall safe, or some other nook."

"Let the police handle this," Ira said.

"I'm helping the police," I said.

"What if the place is being watched?"

"By the police? I think not. Their work is done."

"You're going to just waltz in, are you?"

"I prefer the Texas Two-Step," I said. "I'll get in quick. They won't have the security system hooked up."

"Has it occurred to you that someone may be in the house?"

"I'll be quiet," I said.

"Michael, I must advise against this."

"How about coming with me?"

"Michael—"

"Don't wait up for me. And save my soup."

"Michael!"

I was already halfway to the door.

The Aiken house was dark, of course. The front door lock was easy, and once in I moved around a bit, listening for sounds. Heard none.

Using a flashlight like a trained burglar, I started with the living room. Took me five minutes or so to check behind everything that hung on a wall. An abstract print, a mirror, a framed poster from the movie *Sands of Iwo Jima*, a series of black-and-white photos of driftwood.

Nothing behind them.

There was a built-in bookcase on one side of the room. I felt around the edges, then checked the shelves. I pulled out four or five books at a time, looked, put them back. It was slow going. But I finally got to the last shelf. It held one thick volume that I took out by itself—William Shirer's *The Rise and Fall of the Third Reich*.

It was a good choice because it saved my life.

The floor creaked behind me. I turned just in time to see a shadow bearing down on me, about to strike.

I held the Shirer book out like a shield.

A knife thrust into it.

The momentum of the attacker pushed me against the shelf. Instinct drove my right elbow into the attacker's face. A perfect blow. Down he went.

The knife was sticking out of the book. I tossed it aside.

I knelt and grabbed the guy by the shirt, pulled him up. I still had my flashlight in my right hand. I lit up the guy's face.

His eyes were rolling around. And the eyes belonged to Sammie Sand.

I set the flashlight on the floor and slapped him.

He groaned.

I slapped him again.

"Who sent you?" I said. "Talk now or it's gonna be a long—"

Blam.

Gunshot, from somewhere in the room. I felt it wham into Sammie Sand's back.

I dropped him and dove. Two shots hit the bookshelf.

I rolled, got up, and ran to where I thought a door was.

I remembered correctly. I was in another room. I put my back to the wall just inside the door.

And waited.

Listened.

Looked in the dim for something to use as a weapon.

"Michael?"

Ira's voice!

"Ira, there's a shooter!"

"No, dear boy. The shooter is out here. Out cold."

I stepped out of the office and made my way to the front door. Ira was standing there.

T he form was laid out on the front lawn.

"Had no choice," Ira said, holding up one of his braces.

"You came."

"I wasn't about to let you get into trouble. I saw the first one enter, then the second. Then heard the shots. I caught this one in the kisser coming out."

"Your timing is exquisite." I knelt down and, in the soft moonlight, looked at the face of the shooter.

All breath left me.

"I didn't suspect it would be a woman," Ira said.

"Not just any woman," I said. "Her name is Holly Samara."

"The DEA agent?"

"The very same."

"Here," Ira said, holding out a long, plastic zip tie. "Secure her wrists behind her while I call the police."

. . .

After I tied her up she started to come around. I pulled her to a sitting position.

It took her a few seconds to realize where she was.

She winced in pain. Shook her head.

And then she smiled at me.

"Hello, Mike," she said.

"Holly."

"I suppose you're wondering..."

"Yeah," I said.

"We could have been great together," she said.

"You were setting me up from the start, from that little meet-cute downtown."

"I refuse to answer," she said.

"And you recruited Sammie Sand just to take special care of me."

"Get me a lawyer."

"They'll catch up with Adrian Hart, you know."

"Who is Adrian Hart?" she said with a smirk.

"Why Holly? Just why?"

"I'll see you again, Mike. Someday I'll see you and we'll talk."

She looked in my eyes with a confidence that sent a chill through me. She said not another word.

When it was all over—the scene, the cops, the statements—I drove back to Ira's in my rental. It occurred to me that Holly Samara or Sammie Sand put a tracker on it while I was enjoying matzo ball soup a few hours earlier.

Ira helped me locate the device with an electronic scanner. He looked at it and said, "Nice workmanship. Not as nice as mine, but it did its job."

My mind was still reeling. "I need a beer."

We sat in the backyard. The air was cool and the night sky typical of Los Angeles—a few stars visible, the brighter ones blinking like celebrities on a red carpet as the dimmer lights watched from behind the ropes.

Presently, Ira asked, "Have you made a decision yet?"

"Decision?"

"About becoming a monk."

I spotted Orion's Belt in the heavens. "Somehow, I don't think I'm cut out for the holy life."

"So you're going to stay?"

"Where would you be without me?" I said.

"That's nice to hear," Ira said. "And, I might add, it's the other way around, too."

I was about to give him a snappy answer, but it caught in my throat.

"What's wrong, my good friend?" Ira said.

"I don't know," I said. "Could be some of that ice ring is melting."

"You think?"

"I only said could be."

Ira put his hand on my shoulder. "Thanks for letting me know." After a beat he added, "Have you thought about telling that to Sophie?"

I shook my head.

"Why don't you?" Ira said.

"I was almost pulled in by her, Ira. Holly, I mean. The deception. She played me like a cheap violin."

"It happens," Ira said.

"It shouldn't. Not to me."

"You are human, Michael. Hate to break it to you."

"Maybe Lucretius was right. Love is madness and misery. Beware that you are not entrapped."

"You don't believe that."

"I don't?"

"No. Forget Holly. Think about Sophie."

"That's a lot to think about," I said.

"When in the history of the world has there not been a lot to think about?"

"Our curse," I said.

"Our opportunity," Ira said. "Why don't you take the opportunity and call her?"

"When?"

"Now."

"You are one pushy rabbi," I said.

"I prefer the word charming," Ira said. He got up, grabbed his braces, and started for the house.

"Can we watch *Horsefeathers*?" I said.

"I'll make the popcorn," Ira said.

I laced my hands behind my head and looked at the sky for a while. A police helicopter chopped by without stopping to circle the neighborhood. Time to be thankful for the little things.

I took out my phone. For a full minute I looked at it as if it was some ancient seer stone holding the great answers of life and all I had to do was wait for them.

Then I got tired of waiting.

And made the call.

AUTHOR'S NOTE

Many thanks for reading Romeo's Town. I greatly appreciate it. Added appreciation would come if you would kindly leave a review on the Amazon site.

The Mike Romeo Thriller Series
(in order)
1. Romeo's Rules
2. Romeo's Way
3. Romeo's Hammer
4. Romeo's Fight
5. Romeo's Stand
6. Romeo's Town

MORE THRILLERS FROM JAMES SCOTT BELL

The Ty Buchanan Legal Thriller Series

#1 Try Dying
#2 Try Darkness
#3 Try Fear

"Part Michael Connelly and part Raymond Chandler, Bell has an excellent ear for dialogue and makes contemporary L.A. come alive. Deftly plotted, flawlessly executed, and compulsively readable. Bell takes his place as one of the top authors in the crowded suspense genre." - **Sheldon Siegel**, *New York Times* bestselling author

The Trials of Kit Shannon Historical Legal Thrillers

Book 1 - City of Angels
Book 2 - Angels Flight
Book 3 - Angel of Mercy
Book 4 - A Greater Glory
Book 5 - A Higher Justice

Book 6 - A Certain Truth

"With her shoulders squared and faith set high, Kit Shannon arrives in 1903 Los Angeles feeling a special calling to practice law ... Packed full of genuine, deep and real characters ... The tension and suspense are in overdrive ... A series that is timeless!" — **In the Library Review**

Stand Alone Thrillers

Your Son Is Alive
Long Lost
Blind Justice
Don't Leave Me
Final Witness
Framed
Last Call

Mallory Caine, Zombie-At-Law Series

You read that right. A new genre. Part John Grisham, part Raymond Chandler—it's just that the lawyer is dead. Mallory Caine, Zombie at Law, defends the creatures no other lawyer will touch...and longs to reclaim her real life.

Pay Me In Flesh
The Year of Eating Dangerously
I Ate The Sheriff

ABOUT THE AUTHOR

 **James Scott Bell** is a multi-bestselling author of thrillers and books on the writing craft. He is a winner of both the International Thriller Writers Award and the Christy Award (Suspense). He attended the University of California, Santa Barbara, where he studied writing with Raymond Carver, and graduated with honors from USC Law School. He lives and writes in Los Angeles.

JamesScottBell.com